DUDLEY PUBLIC LIBRARIES

The loan of this book may be renewed if not required by other readers, by contacting the library from which it was borrowed.

Also by S. E. Durrant

LITTLE BITS OF SKY

Shortlisted for the Branford Boase Award 2017
Shortlisted for the UKLA Book Awards 2017
Nominated for the CILIP Carnegie Medal 2017

"This remarkable debut novel reads as if written by an experienced children's author at the height of her powers… This is an uplifting and convincing evocation of time and place, of two vivid young lives, and of the hope that kindness can offer."
The Sunday Times, Children's book of the week

"This blew me away, what a very special debut. Tender, heartbreaking and ultimately uplifting."
Fiona Noble, The Bookseller

"*Little Bits of Sky* is a truly, truly, truly lovely story. It is completely comfortable in its own skin from the first page to the last … feeling deeply authentic and real. Uplifting and heartwarming without ever being twee, this debut will find a place in the heart of readers of any age."
The Bookbag

"What makes it even more special is how Durrant keeps it realistic but maintains a sense of hope and optimism. A must-read."
BookTrust

"So good and fresh and believable."
Emma Chichester Clark

"…a beautiful book … the characters are brilliantly drawn. I can offer no higher compliment than that this is worthy of Elizabeth Laird at her very best."
The Scotsman

For the teachers and children
I have met along the way

First published in the UK in 2020 by Nosy Crow Ltd
The Crow's Nest, 14 Baden Place,
Crosby Row, London SE1 1YW

Nosy Crow and associated logos are trademarks and/or registered
trademarks of Nosy Crow Ltd

Text © S. E. Durrant, 2020
Cover and inside illustrations © Rob Biddulph, 2020

3 5 7 9 10 8 6 4 2

A CIP catalogue record for this book is available from the British Library

Printed and bound in Great Britain by Clays Ltd, Elcograf S.p.A.
Typeset by Tiger Media

Papers used by Nosy Crow are made from wood grown in
sustainable forests.

ISBN: 978 1 78800 470 1

www.nosycrow.com

I
October
THE LOST GIRL

The lost girl looks like me. Even though she's two and I'm nearly eleven. She's got the same wavy hair and gappy teeth and her hair could be red like mine, though it's hard to tell in a black-and-white photo. You just have to guess. (My guess is it's red.) The photo's bent at the edges as if it's been carried around in someone's pocket and the corners got turned over. The girl's wearing a short-sleeved dress with a white collar and she's standing on the stones on Brighton beach with the West Pier in the background (the pier that burned down).

She might be smiling but she's also squinting as if she's got the sun in her eyes or maybe an eyelash. I can't really tell. All I know is on that day, whenever it was, she stood on the beach with a bucket at her feet and an ice cream in her hand. Looking like me. There could be a seagull hovering out of sight waiting to dive-bomb her ice cream, or she might have let the ice cream drip down her wrist because she never liked it in the first place. She just held it for the photo. Or it might have been the best ice cream she ever tasted.

Mimi pulled her out of a box of old photos and propped her on the mantelpiece next to the bracelet. She called her the lost girl.

Every now and then, if we leave the window open or if someone walks in the door, the photo flutters on to the carpet.

On the back it says *Coral*.

Bad things, good things

My name's Iris and my grandma's name's Mimi. And that's what I call her. The whole family does. I know some people think it's weird but it's not weird for me or my mum or even the two-year-old twins. I've been staying with her for five weeks. If I could stay here forever,

I would. I've got my mum's old bedroom all to myself and there's no damp or black mould crawling across the walls like in my real bedroom. There's no water seeping in at the corners either, and even though the room's full of Mimi's stuff I don't mind at all.

Other good things are:

There's a seagull living on the roof.

I don't have to see my dad pull his hair out while he looks at the mould in my bedroom.

I don't have to hear my heart pound when the twins pull the radiator off the wall or think they can fly by jumping off the kitchen table (yes they've done both).

And I don't have to watch my mum run out of the door eating a slice of toast because she's late for work and spend the whole day worrying she might have choked on her way to the hospital (she's a doctor) and there'll be no one there to do the Heimlich manoeuvre. (The Heimlich manoeuvre, in case you're wondering, is what you do when someone's choking. I learned it after one of the twins tried to swallow a Christmas bauble.)

Even though Mimi's house is not far from mine, living here is the opposite of living at home. We eat when we feel like it, we talk when we feel like it, we listen to each other. We bake cakes. We make a mess. And we sit on the sofa and look at her millions of photos from when she

3

was a photographer. It's a ten-minute walk to the beach. These are the good things.

The not-so-good things are: the shower's cold, I don't always get breakfast, things go missing. But that's mostly it! More good than bad.

Mimi's seagull

Our seagull always calls twelve times – *kee-yah kee-yah kee-yah kee-yah kee-yah kee-yah kee-yah kee-yah kee-yah kee-yah kee-yah kee-yah* – then takes a breath. I'm calling our seagull *her* because you can't really tell with seagulls. Not unless they lay an egg. And there's no egg. Not this year anyway. She's my new, non-human friend.

I communicate with our seagull telepathically. I'm pretty sure she understands. I think she's trying to tell me my life will be perfect when I'm twelve.

I've been trying to work out if other seagulls call the same number of times but I've noticed they don't. Our seagull's special. The seagull on Lee and Danny's roof over the road calls eight times, ten times or sixteen times (all even numbers). That might mean something – I've no idea. Then again, it might be lots of different seagulls. I only know ours. And if you're wondering how I know ours, all I can tell you is it's something to do with the way she tilts her head. And the look in her eyes.

The seagulls on the beach cry any number of times. The most I've heard is one hundred and thirty-eight times from two seagulls circling a family eating chips. (Yes really!) It's probably a record.

Bungee jump

I'm sitting on the step in Mimi's little back garden, watching the seagull watching me from the top of the shed, when a voice says, "Have you ever done a bungee jump?"

A boy's peering over the top of the hedge.

"Have you? Have you?" he says.

I shake my head.

"I'm going to do one when I'm old enough," he says. "It's going to be one of my challenges."

I look away but he carries on.

"I thought it was just an old woman who lived there," he says.

I grit my teeth. If I don't speak to him, maybe he'll stop talking. He doesn't.

"I thought it was just a crazy old woman who talks to the moon."

"She's not crazy," I say, "and she's not just an old woman. She's my grandma, if you want to know. And she's called Mimi. And I live here too."

"OK," he says. "I'm coming through."

He drops out of sight and a stick followed by two hands pushes through a gap in the bottom of the hedge. Then comes curly black hair with leaves caught in it and a pair of glasses falling off a nose and behind them a face all screwed up and concentrating. He stands up and shakes himself down.

"We're in the same class," he says, "you and me. I'm Mason."

I know he's Mason. He's the boy who started my school two weeks ago, who throws paper aeroplanes across the room when Miss Sharma's not looking, who tells jokes no one laughs at and walks out of school alone.

And now he's my neighbour.

Mason

Mason stays forever, poking at things with his stick, talking about his mum and her driving lessons and his hobby collecting marbles and his new room. The seagull gets bored and flies up on to the chimney. If I could fly up there myself, I would.

Eventually I say, "I'm going in now."

Just like that. Quite rude really. I watch out of the kitchen window as Mason waits for a few minutes then crawls back through the hedge. As soon as he's gone the seagull flies back down to the shed and screeches. Twelve times.

Here's what I learned about Mason:

He just moved next door with his mum who works as an accountant for a big company, which means she's always, always, always in the office or working at home (Mason's words). And his mum's brilliant with numbers (Mason's words). He says you can give her any numbers and she can add them up or divide them or multiply them. All in her head. He's pretty impressed with his mum.

His bedroom is next to mine. They both look on to the little back gardens and we have the same flat roof outside our rooms. He says if we want we can meet on the flat roof sometimes. (I don't want.)

He can't stay still, even for one moment.

He goes to the flea market every week to look for marbles (his grandad gave him his first one).

His grandad's very old now. Mason says he's losing his marbles. (He thought this was really funny and explained he didn't mean real marbles. I think I'd already worked that out.)

He wants us to walk to school together and go to the market together and do lots of things together. (I don't want to do anything with him.)

He thinks Mimi's garden and his garden is just one garden with a hedge down the middle.

That means he thinks it's his.

Me and the seagull

"Have you made a new friend?" says Mimi.

"No."

"Oh, that's a shame," she says. "Just I saw you talking to that boy."

I shrug.

"Not wanting to be rude," she says, "but you could do with a friend."

"That is rude," I say. "And anyway, you're my friend. You and the seagull."

She wraps her arms round me. She smells of her special purple soap.

"That's very sweet," she says, "but wouldn't you like a friend your own age? And species?"

She's laughing.

"Ha ha," I say. "Not really."

"Well, aren't we lucky then?" she says. "Me and the seagull."

And she digs her fingers into my ribs and tickles me, so even though I'm annoyed I can't be annoyed for long.

Interesting things about Mimi

My dad calls Mimi a live wire. My mum rolls her eyes when he says this because Mimi's her mum and maybe it was no fun growing up with a live wire. Because a live wire is full of electricity and jumps around all over the place and if you're not careful it can give you an awful shock. Dad doesn't mind, though. He's an electrician when he's not looking after the twins. He knows how to handle it. And I don't mind either. It makes life interesting.

Anyway, things about Mimi:

Small.

Very thin.

Gappy teeth like me (and Coral).

Long white hair – it used to be brown. (Me and Mum got the red hair.)

Patterned scarf in her hair or round her shoulders.

Wears earrings – sometimes dangly ones, sometimes shiny studs.

Likes bright dresses with patterns.

Wears yellow sandals in summer and red ankle boots in winter and pink slippers in the house.

Messy. Mum says very messy. Mimi has stuff everywhere and she likes it. (I like it too actually.)

Puts ribbons on things – kitchen drawers, baskets, her apron, her swimming costume, her finger.

Moves like a bird – fast, like she might be about to take off. If she had wings, I don't think she'd ever come down from the sky.

Every now and then she does a little dance. In the kitchen, in the living room, in the street. (Yes, it's embarrassing.)

Her face usually goes up – smile, eyebrows – but when it goes down it goes down a very long way and she looks about a hundred years old.

Loves to swim in the sea. She's done it since she was a little girl.

A bit forgetful.

Likes to laugh.

Her most precious thing is the bracelet she keeps on the mantelpiece. Her dad made it for her before he was killed in the war. He sent it home to Brighton when Mimi was four years old. Mimi says it's worth nothing and everything all at the same time. It's got five red wooden beads, three metal beads and a small green metal whistle and they're threaded on to a bit of string with a knot you can tighten.

Oh, another thing about Mimi is she wants to sort all her photos before she dies.

I said, "You're not going to die soon, are you?"

And she said, "Not if I can help it."

2
REALLY HONESTLY TRULY

I'm the only one in my family who doesn't like swimming in the sea. Even the twins like it. So long as they've got enormous towels and lots of snacks and someone to make a fuss of them when they get cold. But I don't like it at all. I especially hate it when my feet can't touch the ground because I don't know what's hiding there.

When I was little I told my dad there was a monster in the sea. I used to tell him everything. And he said there was really honestly truly nothing to worry about. He actually said it like that – really honestly truly. He said in

Brighton you get mackerel and seagulls and you might even see a seal, but he'd never seen a shark or even heard of one.

And after that every time we went in the sea he would chase me with his hands like jaws and then he would lift me on to his shoulders so the shark couldn't get me. But to be honest I didn't exactly think there was a shark. I just felt sure there was something hiding under the water, waiting to grab me. And even now I'm older I still believe that. Because, really honestly truly, how could anyone ever really know there isn't?

Jam on scrambled eggs

Mimi's got a blue ribbon tied round her finger and a flowery scarf holding up her hair. She's about to drop a spoonful of strawberry jam on to my scrambled egg and I'm about to stop her when Mason appears in the garden. When he sees us he freezes. He's got that look my dad calls "rabbit in the headlights" – like when the twins were caught eating a tub of ice cream under the bed.

I wave the ketchup at Mimi but it's too late. She plops the jam on to my egg and opens the kitchen door. Mason tries to make himself invisible by standing completely still, but he's wearing a big woolly red jumper and his glasses are lopsided. It doesn't work.

"Welcome," says Mimi. "Come in and have some breakfast."

I can tell Mason doesn't want to come in, but before he knows it he's sitting at the kitchen table and Mimi's picking four hedge leaves out of his hair. She lays them on the table in a line. Mason picks them up and puts them in his pocket.

"Thanks," he grunts.

I give Mimi a look (meaning don't encourage him to stay) but she ignores me.

"Nice to meet you," she says. "I'm Mimi. Scrambled eggs?"

Mason shakes his head.

Mimi's hair is slowly falling out of its scarf and her glasses are sliding down her nose. It's not a relaxing look.

"Juice?" she says.

Mason shrugs. Mimi pours him some juice.

"So," she says, "you must be…?"

"Mason," says Mason.

And that's the end of the conversation. Mimi eats toast and jam very slowly, I push my egg and jam round my plate, and Mason taps the table with his fingers and takes lots of little sips of juice, like maybe twenty sips in a row without taking a breath. And all the time his eyes are searching the room, looking at the old pots and pans and dusty eggcups and the ribbons tied to the kitchen drawers and the mugs with things like *Life is better at the beach* written on them and *Good things come in waves*.

When Mimi's finished her toast she says, "Mason, would you like to come to the beach with us? We're going swimming."

Mason looks surprised. "Today?" he says.

Mimi nods. "It's very invigorating," she says. "Liven you up."

I'm thinking Mason livened up would be especially annoying. Luckily he's not keen.

"No thanks," he says. "It's bit cold for me."

When Mimi goes upstairs he whispers, "Is that jam on your egg?"

"Yes," I say. "What about it?"

"Nothing," he says.

"It's delicious actually," I say.

"You're eating it very slowly," he says.

Then he gulps down his juice, slides under the table and darts back into the garden. When he's gone I scrape what's left of the eggs and jam (which is most of it) into the bin.

Swimming

Mimi's waiting at the front door. She's carrying one of those old-fashioned baskets, the sort people used to use if they were picking apples. There's a blue ribbon tied round the handle, like the one on her finger. Two towels are folded on top.

"Let's go, Iris," she says.

She's wearing trainers and a green knitted dress with roses on it and a big purple knitted jumper with wool coming loose at the sleeves and a green hat and silver hoops in her ears. And she's doing a little tap dance. I'm wearing a fleece, T-shirt and jeans and I'm walking in slow motion. I'm hoping if I'm slow enough, Mimi might change her mind.

As soon as we're out of the house I'm shivering. The sky's blue with little white clouds and the sun's shining but it's really cold. This is absolutely, one hundred per cent the last time I swim in the sea this year.

We walk down Mimi's little path and she turns up the lane towards the flea market.

"Aren't we going to the beach?" I say.

"Yes," she says and keeps walking.

"The other way then," I say, and I tap her on the shoulder.

She hesitates for a moment then laughs. "Of course," she says.

And she turns round. As we walk back past the house Mimi's neighbour Lee appears in his front garden across the road and shouts, "Beautiful morning!"

We wave.

The seagull calls from the top of the house. Twelve times. Mimi does another little dance and (because Lee's gone back inside) I do one too. Don't ask me why. Just because.

Bracelet

Streams of cars race along the road that stretches along the seafront. Mimi grabs my hand at the traffic lights as if she has to hold me back (she doesn't). I'm as tall as she is but I don't mind. It reminds me of being little. Her hands are cold and bony and our shoulders tap. Something jangles on her wrist.

"You're wearing your bracelet," I say.

"Yes," she says. "I was in the mood."

She's taken it off the mantelpiece and tied it round her wrist.

"Is it a special occasion?" I say.

"I suppose so," she says.

Then she smiles. "Everything with you is a special occasion."

The beach

The wind from the sea creeps under my clothes and into my bones. A woman hurries along the beach with her collar up, her hands shoved into her pockets. Two dogs circle her, yapping. No one's swimming. It's far too cold for normal, sensible people. A man carries a *Fish and Chips* sign out of a café, then stops to gaze at the sea. Two boys wheel stands of postcards and magnets, buckets and spades on to the promenade. A woman in joggers and a jumper is setting up the stripy deckchairs. Seagulls swoop and scramble around the bins.

Mimi waves at the deckchair woman, who shouts back, "Nice morning!"

The sea is perfect sparkling blue. The wind farm looks like a line of spinning matchsticks stretching across the horizon. White foam laps on to the beach. If you saw it without actually being here (like if you were looking at a postcard), you might think it was the middle of summer when, in fact, it's October.

We sit close to the shore. Two seagulls circle above us hoping we've got food. (We haven't.) Suddenly

Mimi's worried.

"I shouldn't have brought it," she says.

"What?"

"My bracelet," she says. "What if I lose it?"

"You won't lose it," I say. "I'll put it in my sock."

She's looking up at the seagulls as if they might dive down, grab the bracelet and carry it across the sea to France.

"It's OK really," I say. "I'll hide it."

She doesn't look reassured.

We peel off our clothes, put on our flip-flops and sit shivering in our costumes with towels round our shoulders. Mimi's got blue ribbons on her costume and they flutter in the wind. I take her bracelet, drop it into one of my socks and put it at the bottom of the basket.

Suddenly Mimi jumps up, pulls on her goggles and marches across the stones in a deliberate waddling walk. She thinks it's funny. It was funny when I was five. Now it's a bit embarrassing.

"Come on!" she shouts.

She kicks off her flip-flops, wades into the sea and ducks down as if she's plunging into a warm bath. I don't understand it at all. I don't even know how a thin old woman can jump into freezing water without turning to ice and floating to the surface like an ironing board.

And I especially don't know how she can do it smiling. But she does. She looks like she's splashing in a bowl of perfectly warm hot chocolate. Like she's in absolutely the best place in the world.

"Come on, Iris," she shouts. "It's fine once you're in."

I follow her down to the shore, kick off my flip-flops and tiptoe into the sea. When it's up to my waist I take a deep breath and plunge in. Water shoots up my nose and down my throat. When I'm not screaming out loud I'm screaming inside.

"Keep moving!" shouts Mimi. "You'll warm up."

She's laughing. "You're made of water," she shouts. "This is where you belong!"

(It doesn't feel like it.)

I swim over to her, my whole body shaking. It's so cold it hurts. The only thing I like about this moment is being next to Mimi. Everything else is horrible – the cold, the hugeness of the sea, the way it gets deeper and deeper and I can't see what's underneath.

We swim together for a while, not far from the shore. I keep close to Mimi in case something's hiding under the water but after a while I stop thinking about the sea monster and whether my feet can touch the ground and for a few minutes something nice happens. I can't exactly say I warm up, I just get used to the cold, but suddenly all I'm thinking about is me and Mimi swimming side by side, our arms moving in time, while white bubbles burst around us.

Air traffic control

Mimi stays in the sea much longer than me. When I've had enough (like after three minutes) I swim to the shore, put on my flip-flops and run back to our basket. Cold water's dripping down my neck. My teeth are chattering. I'm not sure I've ever been this cold. I get dressed as quickly as I can, tie Mimi's bracelet round my wrist and shove my feet into my socks and shoes.

More people are arriving at the beach. A toddler in a pointed pixie hat is chasing a seagull, her dad close behind her in case she runs into the sea. He looks happy, then stressed, then happy again. A family sits on the stones drinking coffee out of paper cups. Seagulls bob on the water or fly in circles overhead. The deckchairs are all empty.

Mimi's getting smaller in the distance, a tiny shape against the blue. She swims in the same direction every time, parallel to the beach heading towards the Palace Pier, and when she gets to a certain point she turns round and swims back.

Mimi's swum in the sea all her life. I know because I've seen the photos. There's a black-and-white photo of her as a little girl on Brighton beach, a towel round her shoulders, gappy teeth, laughing. And there are colour photos of her as a young woman with my grandad (who died before the twins were born), both smiling. Grandad with his funny moustache and Mimi never quite in focus. There are photos of Mum on the beach as a little girl too with Mimi, Mum with her red hair like mine, standing completely still, and Mimi out of focus because she can never stay still for even a moment.

I watch Mimi turn back in my direction and then swim in towards the shore. When the water's waist-deep she wades out of the sea, walks across the stones and puts on her flip-flops. Then she stands for a few moments. Just waiting. I shout but she doesn't hear me so I jump up and stretch out my arms like I'm air traffic control telling a plane where to land. She sees me, waves and marches towards me.

"Wonderful swim," she says. "Wonderful!"

She's so cold even her smile's shivering. Seawater drips from her ribbon round her finger. She pulls off her goggles, dries herself and changes into her clothes. I tie the bracelet round her wrist and as I do I see *MB* carved in tiny letters into one of the red beads.

"Is that you?" I say.

"Yes," says Mimi. "Mimi Butterworth. That was my name."

Then she puts her arms round me and holds me tight.

3
PADDLING POOL

We hear the twins before we see them. We're meeting near the paddling pool. Noah's standing with his feet wide apart as if they're glued to the ground, his arms folded angrily.

He's shouting, "Not coming! Not coming!"

Pearl's running towards us, her mouth wide open. She sounds like she's swallowed a seagull and it wants to get out. Mum's mouth is a little flat line and there's another between her eyes, going up instead of across. Dad picks up Noah and runs towards me.

"Iris!" he says.

He hugs me then Mimi.

"Lovely to see you. How's things?"

"Good," I say.

Pearl screams until I lift her up. Then she takes a breath and screams some more. She's hurting my ears.

"What a horrible noise," I say.

She digs her nose into my neck. It's cold and snotty.

"You look cold, sweetheart," says Mum and before I know it she's taken off her coat and wrapped it round me and Pearl.

It's embarrassing. I pull it off.

"Don't catch a cold," she says. "You're going blue."

"I like blue," I say. "It's my favourite colour."

"How's work on the mould going?" says Mimi.

"Slowly," Dad begins.

I don't want to hear any more. I don't want to even think about going back to the house and all that chaos. I put Pearl down and prod her.

"Come on," I say. "I'll race you!"

Noah clambers down from Dad's arms and the three of us run across the stones.

Not too homesick?

Mimi and the twins are in the paddling pool. If it wasn't for the way they look, it would be hard to tell who's youngest. Mimi's pretending she's about to fall but looking like she actually might. Pearl's jumping up and down and Noah looks like he's standing on the edge of a raging sea that's about to swallow him up. The water's about six inches deep.

Me, Mum and Dad lean on the fence, watching.

"Nice just the three of us, isn't it?" Mum says. "Like the old days."

She kisses the top of my head.

And it is nice.

"So," says Dad. "Not too homesick?"

"I'm fine," I say.

"Call if you've got a problem, won't you?" he says.

"Actually," I say, "the shower doesn't heat properly. Can you fix it? Mimi doesn't mind but I do. She never gets cold."

"OK," says Dad. "Anything else?"

"Yes, I need a new phone," I say. "Mine's rubbish. It's got no storage."

"You can still call, though, can't you?" Dad says. "And Mimi's got a landline."

"Yes, but it's not good for anything else."

"You're ten years old," says Mum. "Why do you need a phone? Live in the real world. Or do some daydreaming."

(This is particularly annoying. I don't think Mum has ever daydreamed in her life.)

"Secondary school," says Dad. "You'll get one then."

I'm about to make a fuss when Pearl trips and lands face down in the water. She's wearing dungarees and they blow up like a balloon. She couldn't be wetter if she tried. She might as well roll around a bit just to get the last little corners fully soaked.

Dad jumps up. Mum rolls her eyes. Pearl hesitates for a moment then screams.

And that's the end of the conversation.

Someone else's family

By the time Pearl's dry and wrapped in Mum's coat, Noah's cold and wants to go home. Mum looks cold too. She's turning my favourite colour. We walk a little way along the beach then wave them goodbye.

As we watch them go I imagine they're someone else's family – the tired woman with the wet girl on her shoulders and the tired man playing tag with the little

27

boy. I imagine I've never seen them before and think how lucky it is there's not an older girl trailing behind them (me in a parallel life). Then I put my arm through Mimi's and we walk towards the remains of the West Pier.

The West Pier

There are two piers in Brighton. The Palace Pier is still open and has slot machines and rides and fish and chips. The West Pier's the one that burned down. There's an observation tower on the beach next to where the West Pier used to be. It's a massive stick poking into the sky with a huge glass pod like a ring doughnut that moves slowly up and down. People pay for rides in the pod so they can look at the view. As we walk towards it the pod's going up. An old couple gaze out at the sea. A family press their faces to the glass and a girl in a pushchair looks down at us and sticks out her tongue. Mimi sticks her tongue out back and the girl smiles.

All that's left of the West Pier is twisting brown metal rising out of the water like a skeleton. All the wood and glass and buildings and rides have gone. Seagulls fly in circles overhead or perch on the metal. A small boat bobs on the horizon.

"What did the pier used to be like," I say, "before it burned down?"

Me asking Mimi about the West Pier is one of our traditions. I always ask the same question and she always gives the same answer.

"Well," she says, " there was a bathing station where you could get changed and dive into the sea and then climb back on to the pier again and there was a helter skelter and a restaurant. And I met your grandad on the pier. He was coming out of the fortune teller's."

"What did the fortune teller say?"

"Well, your grandad asked if he would ever fall in love and she said yes but he'd have to wait years. Then he dropped his change coming out of her kiosk and I bumped into him as he picked it up. And that's how we met. And when the pier caught fire we sat here on the stones and watched clouds of yellow smoke fill the sky. The pier was already abandoned but it was such a sad sight. Every day we would come down and another bit would have fallen into the sea."

She sighs. "But even now it's my favourite place in all of Brighton. I have a lot of happy memories here."

It's hard to imagine the pier as a living thing, full of people and things happening.

"It's still beautiful, don't you think?" Mimi says.

I know we're looking in the same direction at the same thing, but I'm sure we're seeing something different. It does look beautiful, though, like a creature rising up out of the sea, and not at all scary because it's only a skeleton.

Coral

When we get home the photo of Coral's fluttered on to the carpet. Mimi picks it up.

"Who was Coral?" I say. "Why do you call her the lost girl?"

Mimi sighs. "She was my cousin," she says. "She was lost at sea."

My heart does a little painful jolt. I'm not exaggerating. It's like an electric shock runs right through me.

"She was on a pleasure cruise with her parents just after the war," Mimi says. "It was the first trip of the season and the boat wasn't seaworthy. She was two years old."

My heart does about a million flips. If it could scream it would be going AARGGH! I feel as though I've known about Coral all of my life and I was just waiting for someone to tell me. I imagine the sea monster tipping the boat over and eating Coral all those years ago. I try to speak but nothing comes out.

I take a breath and try again. "Did your aunt and uncle drown too?" I say.

Mimi nods. "Yes, my father's brother and his wife. All three gone. My mother's heart must have absolutely broken. My father had died in the war the previous year so she was all alone. Apart from me."

"Where did it happen?"

"Just a few miles down the coast."

She sighs. "This photograph," she says, "is full of ghosts. Coral's gone and so has the West Pier."

"And the person who took the photo," I say.

"Almost certainly," says Mimi. "It was nearly seventy-five years ago."

"Do you miss her?"

"Well," says Mimi, "I was five when she died and she was two, so I'm not sure I remember her. But I missed the idea of her. I didn't have any siblings and she was my only cousin." She smiles.

"She was my imaginary friend when I was a child. I'd chat to her and tell her my stories. Like you chat to the seagull."

"I don't exactly chat to the seagull," I say. "We just understand each other."

"Well," she says, "you wouldn't know then. But an imaginary friend's very handy if you're a lonely child."

31

I shrug.

"And they don't answer back," she says.

She puts the photo back on the mantelpiece and I go upstairs, sit on my bed and take deep breaths until my heart stops racing. Then I open the window. The seagull's sitting on Mimi's shed, looking up at the sky. I've never spoken to her out loud before (really honestly truly) but now I do. Not loud enough for anyone else to hear but just loud enough for my words to be carried to her on the breeze.

"Coral was eaten by the sea monster," I say.

She looks at me, lifts one leg and scratches her head with her foot. Then she screeches twelve times – *kee-yah kee-yah kee-yah kee-yah kee-yah kee-yah kee-yah kee-yah kee-yah kee-yah kee-yah kee-yah*.

She might be telling me not to worry, everything will be fine when I'm twelve, or she might be saying she wants twelve fish for tea. Anyway, I'm worried. I can't help it.

Shadow

I spend the rest of the day making a lemon cake with Mimi and helping her sort out some photos she took of the West Pier before it fell into the sea. And I almost forget about Coral.

But at night she comes to me in my sleep, weaving through water, tangled in seaweed, reaching out for her falling ice cream. And behind her a shadow gets closer and closer.

4
FACING WEST

My real home, where my family live, is up the hill. If I stand on my toes and look out of the attic-room window, I can see a strip of sea and, if it's not too misty, the wind farm flickering against the sky. I can't see Mimi's house, though. We're not high enough for that.

Mum says the wind is blowing our house down. She says it comes in from the sea and it's been battering our house for a hundred years. That's why mould's creeping into my room and Dad has to fill the holes between the bricks with stuff to keep the rain out.

But apart from the mould our house isn't the most relaxing place anyway because the twins are always screaming and shouting and breaking things and whenever Mum's there she's picking up stuff and putting it away, even if the twins just get it right out again. She's like a human vacuum cleaner.

And if you don't know what it's like to live with a human vacuum cleaner, I'll tell you – it's rubbish (ha ha).

Shipwreck

Mimi's house looks like it's been caught in a shipwreck. There's stuff everywhere. There are beads and bangles hanging on coat hangers, loads of ornaments, old toy cars and dolls, cups and saucers that don't match, piles of books on the floor and falling off shelves and lots of photographs stuffed into boxes. Some of the boxes are bursting, some have broken lids with bits of paper sticking out, some say *This way up* on a sticker that's upside down.

When I moved in Dad carried my case up to Mum's old room and (I'm not exaggerating) he jumped back when he opened the door as if a seal was juggling bananas on the bed. Then he turned to me and smiled and said,

"Hey ho." (Meaning *never mind, let's get on with it.*)

His smile was slipping around his face and it wasn't because he was worried about the twins, because they were happy downstairs watching *Chitty Chitty Bang Bang* with Mimi. It was because we couldn't see the bed for all the boxes piled on top and we couldn't see the floor for all the boxes piled there too.

He lifted the boxes off the bed and Thomas (Mimi's cat) jumped out of a blanket, hissed and ran out of the door. Dad cleared the bed and made space on the shelves for boxes. Any he couldn't find space for he put against the wall so the floor was clear enough to walk across. And, funnily enough, although all that stuff balancing on top of each other would usually make me worry that a sneeze (or an earthquake) might make it collapse, it actually doesn't bother me. In fact, I like it.

Because there's a whole life here all muddled up and there are photos of lots and lots of other lives. And when I go to sleep I imagine all the stories wrapping themselves round me and drifting into my dreams.

How to open the parachute

I've just finished breakfast and I can hear Mimi running up and down the stairs, opening and closing doors. It's like when the twins know there're sweets hidden and they're not going to stop looking until they find them. Finally she bursts into the kitchen and clatters around in here. If her head was loose, it would be spinning.

"What's the matter, Mimi?" I say.

"I've lost something."

"What?"

She shakes her head and flaps her arms. She looks like she's jumped out of a plane and forgotten how to open the parachute.

"I can't remember," she says.

"I'll help you," I say.

"Will you? Will you?"

I nod and nod so she knows I mean it. I must look like my head's about to fall off. I hope Mason's not watching from the garden.

"I'll write things down for you," I say. "And if you lose something or forget something, we can look at my list."

"You'll do that for me?"

"Yes," I say. "If you tell me things you want to remember, I'll write them down."

Mimi's arms stop flapping and slowly the creases drop out of her face. (Not all of the creases. She's old.) It's as though she's drifting gently back to earth, blue sky above her and grass to soften her fall.

"OK," she says. "OK."

She watches me wash my bowl and spoon and pick up my bag.

"Going somewhere nice?" she says.

"School," I say.

She laughs. "Of course," she says. "Is that why you're wearing your uniform?"

I nod. Then she runs out of the kitchen and back up the stairs. Only this time she's smiling.

School

Miss Sharma has rearranged the seats in class and put Mason next to me. I'm not pleased. I give her the same look I gave Mimi when she invited Mason in for breakfast. It doesn't work any better.

"Just a reminder," she says, "that we're going to the museum next week. While we're there I'd like you to think about why visitors to Brighton might want to go to the museum rather than head straight to the beach. What might they see? What's interesting there? Later this term you'll be doing persuasive writing on anything you choose, so this will be good practice."

Mason's making a paper plane under the desk.

"Do you understand that, Mason?" says Miss Sharma.

Mason looks up. "Yes, miss."

"OK," she goes on, "you will be walking to the museum in pairs with the person you sit next to, so there's no need to worry about finding a partner."

Mason looks at me and beams. My heart sinks.

"Lovely," says Miss Sharma. "Now what we have to do this morning is choose a class Eco Rep. That's someone who will help ensure we are doing all we can to protect the environment. Do I have any volunteers?"

Lots of hands shoot up including Mason's. His paper plane drops to the floor.

"Wonderful!" says Miss Sharma. "Mason, I'm going to ask you to be our Eco Rep as you are new to our school and it will be a good way for you to get to know everyone."

Mason stands up and takes a little bow.

"And," says Miss Sharma. She points at the plane. "You could make a very good start by putting that piece of paper in the recycling bin."

Don't you have any friends?

I want to walk home on my own but Mason runs after me.

"Don't you have any friends?" he says.

He's really quite rude.

"What?" I say.

"Well," he says, "I haven't got any friends because I just moved to Brighton but you've been here forever. Where's all your friends? You seem a nice enough person."

(He sounds about a hundred years old.)

I don't think it's any of his business but he's got his face right up to mine so I tell him.

"I've had two best friends," I say, "but they both left. One moved to a different school and the other moved to a different city. I'm not bothered about friends any more if they keep moving. What's the point?"

And then I pull a face, like a how-could-you-not-know face.

"It's hard to move to a new place too," he says. "Take it from me."

"Well," I say, "I'm just going to wait for secondary school and hope I find a friend there who's my sort of person."

"OK," he says. "Thanks very much."

"What do you mean?"

He shrugs. "Don't worry."

He doesn't try to walk with me after that but he's not far behind. I'm trying to avoid standing on a crack and at the same time count how often the seagulls call. It's complicated. Sometimes I think it would be easier if we could split our brain into two compartments. I told Mimi once and she said, "That's what you have other people for – so you can share experiences. You don't have to live entirely in your head."

Anyway, Mason follows me home, humming the whole way. He's really annoying. I step on three cracks and I count two seagulls squabbling. They call sixty-eight times between them without taking a break. I'm hoping the sixty-eight times will make up for me stepping on the cracks and I won't get bad luck.

Chair balancing

Mimi's standing on a chair in my room. She's wearing her pink slippers, the ones that don't have a back (weirdly she calls them mules). The sort you could trip over on the stairs and break your neck.

She wants to get a box of photos off the top shelf. There are boxes on every other shelf but she doesn't want those and she doesn't want the boxes that are stuffed under my bed either. She wants the very highest, hardest to get, have-to-stand-on-a-chair box of photos. I can see her toes curling in her slippers.

"I'll get the box, Mimi," I say.

She shakes her head. "I'm fine thank you," she says. "I'll hand it down."

She grabs the box with both hands and holds it out to me but she looks so shaky my arms spring round her. I can't help it (like Dad when he sees the twins race by).

"Take the box, Iris," says Mimi.

She's beginning to wobble.

I'm trying to decide whether to take the photos or keep holding Mimi when the box slips from her hands. Hundreds of black-and-white photos fall to the floor.

Mimi takes some deep breaths. She might be counting to ten. Then she says, "Can I get down now?"

"I'm really sorry," I say. "I didn't want you to fall."

"Well, I didn't fall, did I?" she says. "So thank you for that."

I clear a path through the photos and she puts her hand on my shoulder and steps off the chair.

"Thank you for the help, Rena," she says.

"I'm Iris," I say. "Rena's my mum."

She doesn't hear me. She's looking at the photos. She kneels down, picks up a handful and throws them into the air. They flutter back down to the floor. Then she begins to laugh.

She looks so funny I'm laughing too.

Photos

We put the photos back in the box, carry them downstairs and tip them on to the kitchen table. Mimi wants to sort them out. They're all photos of weddings. Smiling faces gaze at us, women in white dresses and veils, couples dressed in matching trouser suits. Lots of waistcoats and enormous hats.

"I see these people everywhere," Mimi says. "Sometimes I see a face and I think who is that person and then I remember them clutching a bouquet, even though that might have been fifty years ago and they're probably grandparents by now."

"Haven't you got any colour photos?" I say.

"Yes," she says, "but I printed these in my darkroom. I can't print colour in my darkroom."

"What's a darkroom?"

"It's a place where you make magic," she says. She taps the side of her nose. "I'll show you one day."

She pulls out a photo of two men in white suits, both sprinkled in confetti and carrying bunches of flowers. Both laughing. It's Lee and Danny from over the road. They look younger – Lee with lots of curly hair and Danny tall and strong.

"That was the happiest day of their lives," says Mimi.

I can tell. They look like they just won a million pounds.

Apart from Lee and Danny my favourite photos are:

The fat groom and thin bride who are winking at the camera.

The couple dressed in stripes and eating sticks of rock.

The couple eating hard-boiled eggs while a seagull hovers above them.

The two brides with flowers pinned all over their dresses.

The bride and groom who can't stop laughing. In every photograph one of them is out of focus.

"I took hundreds of that couple," Mimi says. "They couldn't keep still. I had to tell them off in the end."

"Did you?" I say. "On their wedding day?"

"I'm afraid so," she says. "But it was worth it."

She holds up the successful photo – they look like two people who've been made to stand at the back of the class dressed as a bride and groom.

"Did they cheer up afterwards?" I say.

"Oh yes," she says, "when the puppies arrived."

"What do you mean?"

"They brought four puppies to the wedding," says Mimi. "It took me even longer to get a photo with the puppies."

She digs around and pulls out a picture of four puppies with bows in their collars wriggling in the couple's arms. Everyone looks like they're singing, even the dogs.

We throw away photos that are out of focus and some scraps of paper and put the rest back in the box and write *Weddings* on the side.

"Job done," says Mimi. "Thank you, Rena."

"I'm Iris," I say.

"So you are," says Mimi. And she pats my hand.

List

I take the box up to my room and put it back on the shelf. Then I bring down my notebook and pen. I'm in the mood for organising.

"Shall we write the list now?" I say.

"What list?" says Mimi.

"Of things you want to remember."

She looks at me blankly.

"Like we agreed," I say, "in case you forget things."

Mimi shakes her head. "No, sweetheart. It's all fine. Nothing to worry about."

I really want us to write a list so next time she's worried I might be able to help but she's not at all interested.

"There must be something," I say.

45

She shakes her head. "No, no. You are a sweetheart, though," she says.

I write my list anyway.

Notes for Mimi
1. *The girl who is sleeping in the next-door bedroom is called Iris. She is your granddaughter. Rena is Iris's mum (your daughter).*
2. *Iris doesn't like jam on her eggs.*
3. *Turn right when you come out of the house if you want to go down to the sea. If you turn left, you are walking away from the sea. You might even end up at Iris's house.*
4. *Don't take the bracelet out of the house because you might lose it.*
5. *If it's breakfast time and Iris is wearing her school uniform it means she's going to school.*

5
BEST FRIENDS EVER

Mimi's walking the dogs with Lee and Danny. She says they're the best neighbours in the world. Lee went to school with my mum so Mimi's known him for most of his life. This is what they're like:

Lee teaches yoga. He wears a flat cap and he's got a little beard that hangs from the middle of his chin. And he's got a particular way of walking so I can tell it's him even when I see him from the other side of the beach or the end of the road. I can't describe it exactly except to say the air around him moves more slowly than the air round other people. Like the wind can be crashing in off the sea and Lee just walks through it all in his own little tunnel of still air.

He's completely different from Mimi in that way because the air around Mimi never stops moving. If you go into a café with Mimi, the tables wobble and the chairs don't seem big enough, even though she's very small. And her cup of tea usually ends up sloshing into her saucer.

But Lee's always calm. If Lola or Bonnie go missing (they're the dogs), he doesn't imagine them running into the road or disappearing under a wave. He just stops and thinks and decides what to do. I don't know anyone else like him. No one in my family anyway, that's for sure.

Danny's more like Mimi because he's always jumping around. Only he doesn't move in little trembling jolts like a bird looking for worms – he sort of swings around and takes big steps. I always think he's going to knock things over because his elbows are huge but he never does. It's like he's got eyes in the back of his head. He's a headmaster at a junior school (not my school, I'm sorry to say) and I think he must be the best headmaster ever because he's so kind.

If Mimi needs a light bulb changing Danny comes

over and changes it and he won't even need a chair to reach it. He'll just stand on his toes in his enormous shoes and take out the old bulb and put in the new one. And if she hasn't got a light bulb he'll give her one from his house, even if he and Lee might have to sit in the dark. And when the wind blew Mimi's bin over he ran down the street picking up her rubbish, and when one of her shelves came crashing off the living-room wall he screwed it back on so well I don't think it will ever fall off again. In fact, if there was an earthquake, the only thing that would stay up would be Danny's shelf.

Marble hunt

Mason's standing on the front step. He actually rang the doorbell instead of crawling through the hedge. He's got a bag over his shoulder and he's clinking some change in his hand.

"Do you want to come to the flea market?" he says. "I'm on a marble hunt."

I'm not sure if I want to or not so I wait for some more information.

"We can go to my aunt's sweet shop after," he says.

"OK," I say, "I'm coming."

Flea market

It's cold but the sky's perfectly blue. Sun streams down the road, bouncing off mirrors and bits of silver laid on tabletops. Stallholders stand around, chatting and drinking coffee.

I pretended I'm doing Mason a favour by coming but actually I love the flea market. It's a little lane with stalls from one end to the other and you can find every sort of stuff you could ever imagine here. It's like a million old people have left one thing. Most of the stuff is on tables but there are also blankets on the ground covered in books or tools or tennis racquets and board games and things I can't even recognise.

There's an old-fashioned gramophone, which people used to play records on, with a huge speaker like a giant ear on top. A woman's put a record on it and she's dancing around. And there are birdcages with no birds in and old clothes and bits of lace and clocks and furniture and there's stuff called bric-a-brac, which is little bits and pieces people have collected over a lifetime.

Mason's looking in everything in case he might find marbles. He thinks I'm helping him look. I'm not.

He digs a marble out of a pot. "This is a cat's eye," he says. "It's really common, so if you see one don't bother to tell me."

He holds it up to the light. "Look," he says. "You can see the cat's eye."

Three colours twist in the shape of an eye.

I nod.

And then he's off. If he can't find marbles, he goes straight to the next stall. He's really quite boring.

I stop at a table covered in black velvet with lucky charms laid out on top and coins and rings and gold chains and animal ornaments.

A man's sitting in a rocking chair beside the table, eating a boiled egg. He's wearing a long woolly coat and he's dropping the eggshell into a saucer.

"Go on, love," he says. "Anything you like for a pound."

I buy a little black-and-white china cat for Mimi to go with all her other ornaments. It's got a chipped ear so it'll fit her house perfectly. It looks a bit like Thomas (mean and unfriendly). She'll love it.

Mason comes running up, waving a marble as I'm paying.

"Look," he says, "it's a tornado!"

"Is that a good one?" I say.

"Yes! Look!"

He holds it up to the sky. Red and yellow rings circle

51

green. He glances at my cat and I glance at his marble and then we stare at each other, not really interested.

"Right," says Mason. "Sweets!"

Sweets

Mason's aunt's shop is called the Sweet Suite. Mason says "suite" means a set of rooms, though there's only one room as far as I can see. It's a bit confusing, if you ask me.

His aunt's sitting behind the counter scooping sweets out of a jar with a metal spoon and putting them into a striped paper bag. She's got a nose ring and loads of earrings. She smiles when she sees us.

"Hi, Angie," says Mason.

He walks behind the counter and sits on the stool next to her. He looks proud. I have a horrible feeling he might be about to serve me.

"This is my friend, Iris," he says. "Well, she's not actually my friend but she's in my class. She's hoping to find a friend in secondary school."

(He's so embarrassing.)

"Hello," I say.

"Nice to meet you, not-Mason's-friend," says Angie.

She puts down the scoop and seals the bag with a sticker.

"Would you mind watching the shop for a couple of minutes?" she says. "I'm clearing the attic and need to bring some stuff down."

"No problem," says Mason.

He's looking very pleased with himself.

Angie disappears through a door at the back of the shop.

"Those are the other rooms," Mason says. "Her flat's upstairs. It's why we moved to Brighton, because my aunt's here. I'm going to work here when I'm older. I might even get my own shop."

He taps the empty stool. "Come on," he says. "You can help."

I sit down next to him behind the counter. I don't want to be too impressed but I can't help it. Two girls come in with their mum and I pretend it's our shop. I think Mason's doing the same. He's making himself taller. There are mirrors on every wall behind the sweets and I catch sight of us in the mirror opposite. I look eleven and Mason looks about eight.

"I would recommend the toffee," says Mason. "It's the chewiest ever. Unless you've got loads of fillings in which case I'd recommend something soft that won't pull your fillings out. Like marshmallows."

"See," hisses the woman, "I told you about fillings."

"Have you got fillings?" the smallest girl asks Mason.

"No," he says. "Not me."

And he opens his mouth to prove it. We all wince.

"Right," says the woman, "make your minds up, will you?"

I can tell she wants to go.

The girls wander around the shop looking at everything. I'm wishing they would make up their minds because I want us to take the money and give out some change before Angie gets back.

"My assistant here will show you the toffee," says Mason.

The girls look round.

He takes a jar off the counter, picks up some tongs and pulls out a toffee. Then he holds it out to me.

"Am I allowed?"

"Er, yes. It is my aunt's shop. And anyway," he says, "you work here."

He's so proud.

I take a toffee and put it in my mouth but after two chews my teeth lock together. They feel like they're being pulled out of my gums.

The girls get back to choosing and eventually pick

flying saucers and jelly beans. Mason serves them. I can't because I can't speak, which might be why he gave me the toffee. I can't help thinking he's showing off.

When Angie comes back I still can't properly chew. She's carrying two charity bags full of stuff that she puts behind the counter. Then she looks at me.

"Are you OK?" she says.

I nod. I see myself in the mirror. My cheeks are bulging and my eyes look like they're popping out of my head.

"She's trying the toffee," says Mason helpfully. "I told her it's your chewiest ever."

If I wasn't reflected in every mirror on every wall, I'd pull the toffee out and put it in my pocket, but I can be seen from every angle. I just have to keep sucking. Mason talks to Angie about his mum and her driving lessons and the flea market and next week's school trip to the museum. I don't say a word. I can't.

Eventually Angie says, "If you'd like to spit that out, please do."

She hands me a tissue and holds out a bin.

"And choose something to take home," she says, "perhaps not so chewy."

I spit the toffee into the tissue and drop it in the bin. It's embarrassing. I can't quite meet her eye. Then I pick a little bag of Parma violets for Mimi – they're tiny purple sweets and they look like her soap. Actually they taste soapy too. They're her favourites.

Mason chooses gobstoppers, I think because they look like marbles.

Wetsuit

Mimi's in the kitchen with her foot on the table stretching out her aches and pains.

"Old age," she groans.

"I've got you some presents," I say.

I hold out the china cat and the Parma violets.

She puts both feet on the floor and stares at them, smiling.

"What have I done to deserve these?" she says.

We eat some Parma violets and she puts the china cat on a shelf in the living room, next to the clock that's stuck at twenty past four. (Mimi says it tells the right time twice a day.)

Then she says, "Actually I have something for you too."

She hurries upstairs and comes down holding a wetsuit. It's black with red lines down the sides.

"Will it fit you?" she says. "I found it in the back of

the wardrobe. It was your mum's."

"I don't want it, thanks," I say.

"Why not?"

"Because I'm a rubbish swimmer and summer's over, so there's no lifeguards."

I'm not even going to mention the monster. I don't like to think about it.

"You're always safe with me," says Mimi.

I nod but I don't believe it. Not for one second. If there's something in there, it could swallow her in a blink and still be hungry.

The wetsuit goes back in the wardrobe where it will probably stay for another lifetime or until one of the twins wants it.

Hot chocolate

Me and Mimi are going to the beach to watch the sunset. Mimi's making hot chocolate. She pours some into a mug and gives it to me to taste.

"Is it sweet enough?" she says.

I take a mouthful, manage not to throw up, run to the sink and spit it out.

"I think you've put salt in it," I say.

"Salt?"

"Yes, taste it yourself."

She shakes her head. "What a fool I am," she says.

"I might like it another day," I say.

"No you wouldn't," she says. "Don't lie to me."

We make some more hot chocolate, this time with sugar. Mimi doesn't say a word. Then we fill the flask, put on our coats and set off for the beach. As we shut the door behind us Mimi kisses my head, just like Mum does.

"Sorry," she says.

Dog and stick

We sit on the stones and watch the sun sink behind the horizon. It's almost dark. The West Pier looks ghostly against the grey sky. White bubbles roll on to the shore, rattling the stones.

A man with his hood up is walking his dog. He throws a stick and the dog picks it up and returns it, over and over. When the dog sees us he runs over and drops the stick at our feet. It's foamy with spit.

Mimi jumps up and grabs it. "Yuck," she says.

She wipes one hand on her jumper, then she throws the stick high and far. The man and the dog look surprised. Then she sits down again, leans against me and we watch them walk into the distance. Silhouettes of seagulls settle on to the West Pier. In the distance the wind farms dissolve into the darkness.

"The little birds," says Mimi, "what are they called?"

"You mean the starlings?" I say.

"Yes, but what's it called when they all arrive?" she says. She's flapping her hands.

"The murmuration."

She smiles. "Yes!" she says. "The murmuration. I'm looking forward to it."

I love it too. Thousands of starlings come to roost on the West Pier in autumn when the sun goes down. They fly over the sea like huge clouds twisting and turning and changing shape. It's a kind of magic.

"It won't be long," I say.

We drink the hot chocolate and then we play throwing stones into the cup. Sometimes I win and sometimes Mimi does but it doesn't matter. The stones bounce off the beach or tip the cup over or roll down towards the darkening sea.

Notes for Mimi

6. *Don't ask Iris to go swimming again, even in a wetsuit. She doesn't want to go.*
7. *Sugar is nicer in hot chocolate than salt.*

8. *The starlings coming to the beach is called the murmuration.*

Note for me

1. *Don't ever eat toffee from the Sweet Suite, even if it's free and especially if Mason offers it. It's extra chewy and you might choke to death and you might do it in front of a million mirrors.*

6
CAT SANDWICHES

Mimi's making cat sandwiches for my school trip – not filled with cats but shaped like cats. First she fills the sandwich with cheese. Then she presses down with a biscuit cutter in the shape of a cat's head.

"Did you use to do this with Mum?" I say.

"Yes," she says. "Cakes and sandwiches and biscuits. We had so many cutters. Stars and fish and dolphins and birds."

It's hard to imagine Mum doing something so silly.

"Right," she says, "when I've cut the shapes you eat

the crusts. See if you can keep up with me."

It doesn't look very tasty.

"It's your breakfast," she says, "so eat them up."

There's a lot of crust and not much cheese so it's not a very nice breakfast. But the sandwiches look good.

School trip

I'm stuck with Mason and a parent helper who checks her phone all the way to the museum. Mason talks the whole time. I've given up being rude to him or trying to shake him off. I can't really because he's my next-door neighbour. And anyway, his aunt's got a sweet shop.

"What have you got in your sandwiches?" he says.

"Cheese."

"What's your favourite marble?"

"I don't know," I say. "Probably not cat's eyes."

"Do you like galaxies?" he says.

"Which are they?"

"They look like galaxies, duh," he says. "Speckled."

"OK," I say, "yes, maybe galaxies."

"Or how about squids?" he says. "They're the blue ones."

If I don't change the subject, he'll be listing every single marble. So I tell him about Coral and her mum and dad and the boat sinking because nobody checked it was seaworthy. And I'm quite glad to tell him because if I say it out loud maybe Coral will stop coming into my dreams. Because I feel like she's always a shadow behind me.

After that Mason's quiet until we reach the museum.

Museum

The museum is in a big old brick house with black metal gates. Me, Mum and Dad used to come here before the twins were born, when there was time to have fun. Miss Sharma takes us up to the room with the old-fashioned toys and gives us each a pencil and bit of paper.

"Right," she says. "No pushing or running around. There's plenty of time. Enjoy looking at the toys and take a few notes if you'd like to."

We all bundle in and start shoving. The room's exactly as I remember it. There's a vintage car big enough for a child and there are doll's houses and glass cabinets full of old teddies and toys and model aeroplanes and games and marbles. Mason sees the marbles immediately. He spends ages just looking at them. Then he gives his pencil a little chew and starts to write his notes while saying them out loud.

"The museum is a feast of fantastical fun," he says. "Anyone who's ever been a child – or is a child – should visit this marvellous museum." He's looking around to see if anyone's paying attention.

"Everyone was a child once," someone mutters. "Idiot."

Mason shrugs.

I have to walk away in case anyone thinks he's my friend.

I write a few notes of my own:

The museum is a good place for adults to come with a child. But keep toddlers away. Two-year-olds are not welcome, especially twins. If you're going to bring toddlers to Brighton, take them to the paddling pool and make sure they've got a change of clothes. Miss Sharma leans over my shoulder and reads my notes.

"Perhaps be a little less cross," she says.

Lunch

We eat our lunch in the picnic room.

"Are your sandwiches shaped like cats?" says Mason.

"Yes."

"Wow. Who did that? Your grandma?"

I nod.

"Did she put egg and jam in them?"

He's looking around at everyone, hoping they might be interested. They're not. They're all too busy checking each other's lunch to see who got the best. (It's not me.)

"Right," says Miss Sharma when we've eaten. "Put your rubbish in the bin and then you have one hour to explore the museum before we all meet in the foyer at two p.m. for the walk back to school."

"Where you going?" says Mason.

"To look at the cameras," I say. "Because Mimi used to be a photographer."

"Did she?"

"Yes," I say. "And I might be a photographer when I grow up."

(I'm showing off. I can't help it.)

"I'm coming too," says Mason, and he follows me.

Old cameras

Some of the old cameras are taller than people and some of them are a hundred years old. You could never put them in your pocket. People used to have to stand really still to have their photo taken and the photographer had to put a black sheet over his head. I'm wondering how all that equipment can be made small enough to fit into a phone when Mason runs up and pulls at my sleeve.

"I've just seen you in a film!" he says.

"What?"

"Come!" he says. "Follow me!"

He drags me to a tiny theatre with red seats and velvet curtains and a small screen showing old films. He's really excited.

"You'll have to wait," he says. "The film's on a loop."

We sit down next to each other.

There's a black-and-white film of a man in an old-fashioned stripy swimming costume with long shorts and sleeves wading into the sea. In the corner of the film it says *Brighton Beach, 1906*. Girls wearing costumes that look like dresses are paddling in the sea and children in old-fashioned clothes are playing on the beach. Then the film moves through different times until it turns to old-fashioned colour where everything looks brighter and more smudged. In the corner it says *The West Pier, 1954*. It's the West Pier before it burned down. Three men stand at the end of the pier fishing. One turns and smiles at the camera. Small children stand next to them eating ice cream. They wave.

"Watch!" says Mason. "You're next."

The camera's filming the helter-skelter now. Children in shorts and woolly jumpers queue at the bottom of the steps, climb up and then slide down, waving at the camera and running round to do it again. A boy in a blue jumper slides to the bottom, winks and runs off.

And then comes the girl. She's about my age and she's got red hair and she's wearing a green dress and a yellow cardigan. She's going down the slide really fast. When she gets to the bottom she slams her feet on the ground, looks at the camera and smiles. The film freezes on her face. Only it's my face too. Exactly my face. She's even got a gap in her teeth.

"I don't understand," I say.

"I think it means you're a ghost," says Mason. "Wait. It'll come round again."

We watch the film again until we get to *The West Pier, 1954* and the men fishing and the children eating ice cream. And then we see the helter-skelter and the boy in the blue jumper sliding down and then there's the girl. It's like looking at myself in another time. I'm not exaggerating. Imagine seeing yourself dressed in old-fashioned clothes and sitting at the bottom of the helter-skelter on the pier that burned down years before you were born. She has the same red hair as me and the same gappy teeth. It's so confusing.

"That's your ghost," says Mason. "Or maybe you're the ghost and that's the real you."

He's jumping up and down in his seat.

"You probably fell off the pier and now you've come back to haunt us," he says. "You've come to find the person who pushed you off."

If he was a dog he'd be drooling. He's almost dribbling anyway.

I stick out my tongue.

He shrugs. "Now I know why you're so weird," he says.

We watch the reel over and over and every time the girl comes down the slide she still looks exactly like me. When I've watched it eight times I go to find someone who might know about the film. Mason follows. A woman wearing a badge is standing at the top of the stairs talking to a man with a toddler who's looking for the toilets. The toddler's standing in a little puddle. When they hurry off the woman turns to me.

"How can I help?" she says.

"You know that film of the children on the helter-skelter?" I say. "Is it real?"

"Yes it's real."

"Is it acted by modern-day children?"

"No, this is a history museum. It's history."

"Where are those children now?" I say.

"They'll all be grown up by now," she says. "That was

the 1950s."

"Or dead," says Mason.

She nods. "Or dead."

Mason shrugs. "I'm going to the shop," he says.

As he disappears round the corner the woman says, "He's a cheerful soul, isn't he?"

I stare at her for ages hoping she has something else to say but she's noticed the puddle.

"Can I help you with anything else?" she says. "If not, I need a mop."

"No thanks," I say.

Plastic duck

The museum shop is so small if you stood still you could probably reach everything, but Mason still manages to crash around in it. He keeps picking things up and fiddling with them, putting them back, bumping into things. The attendant's eyes flicker towards him. She's sure he's going to break something.

"What are you getting?" I say.

"I wanted marbles," he says, "but they've sold out so I don't know whether to get a pencil sharpener set or a rubber set."

"Which do you need?"

"Neither. I've got both."

"Then don't get them."

"But I've got three pounds," he says.

He picks up a plastic duck and squeezes it. It quacks.

"That's for babies," I say.

My eyes swivel out of the window and down the path. An ice-cream van is parked on the road outside.

"Get an ice cream," I say. "Or two. Get us one each seeing as we're together."

(I haven't got any money.)

"OK," he says.

I follow Mason out of the museum, through the metal gates and on to the pavement. I'm so excited I have to stop my feet doing a little dance. Miss Sharma doesn't notice us go. She's trying to find a coin one of the kids has dropped. She's on her hands and knees searching the floor. The parent helpers are either telling someone off or looking at their phones.

The ice-cream man's drinking a mug of tea. He looks bored and cold. Not many people want ice creams in October.

"How much is a cone?" says Mason.

The man raises his eyebrows and points at the board with the prices. "Three pounds," he says.

"You can get two ice lollies for £1.50 each," I say. "We

can have one each."

Mason shakes his head. "I don't like ice lollies. I want an ice cream."

"Can I have two ice creams for the price of one?" he says. "Seeing as summer's over."

The man shakes his head. "Nope."

"Oh well," says Mason. "Never mind."

He buys a huge scoop of vanilla ice cream in a cone, breaks off the bottom of the cone to make a really small one and scoops a tiny bit of ice cream on to it for me. It wouldn't be enough for a not hungry mouse.

"Thanks very much," I say. "Not."

"You're welcome."

It's not worth licking so I put the whole thing in my mouth. As I do Miss Sharma comes bursting through the doors.

"Iris, Mason! Did I give you permission to leave the museum?"

We shake our heads. Ice cream's dribbling out of the hole in Mason's cone and on to his shoes.

"Did I give you permission to buy ice cream?"

We shake our heads again.

"Inside now!" she yells.

She's furious.

"But I haven't finished," moans Mason. He looks like

he might cry.

I can almost see Miss Sharma's brain whizzing round. She's wondering which would make less mess – taking the dripping cone from Mason or letting him finish it.

"OK," she says. "Iris, you come back inside. Mason, you finish that where I can see you. I'll deal with you both when we get back to school."

She makes Mason stand outside the shop window to eat his ice cream. The whole class watches from inside. He doesn't look like he's enjoying it even a little bit. It's probably the worst ice cream he's ever eaten, though it serves him right. If he'd got us a lolly each we'd have been standing there together and it wouldn't have been embarrassing at all.

"Why's he even allowed one?" someone says.

Everyone's annoyed.

Mason has to walk at the front of the line with Miss Sharma on the way back to school and I have to walk at the back with the parent helper who keeps checking her phone. I think if I turned into a seal and started flapping at her ankles she wouldn't even notice.

I make a seal noise just to see what happens. Nothing happens.

When we get back to school me and Mason have to sit in separate corners (which is actually a relief) and do our writing while everyone else talks about the trip. Mason doesn't look at me the whole time.

When the bell goes he rushes out of the classroom.

"You know you've got ice cream on your shoes," I say as he pushes past me.

"I know," he says. "I wish I'd got the plastic duck."

Cornflakes

I always shout hello when I get home because if Mimi's not in I'm saying hello to the house or the seagull or even Thomas. It's a way of arriving before I'm inside. And this time when I shout hello Thomas comes running, his tail up. Unusually friendly. (This never normally happens.) He's jumping around my feet, purring.

Mimi's asleep on the sofa, a box of photos by her side. I give her a kiss and she opens her eyes.

"Rena?" she says.

"It's me," I say, "Iris. I just got back from school."

"Oh," she says. "Did you have a good day?"

"Yes. We went to the museum."

"Of course you did," she says. "Did you have lunch?"

"Cheese sandwiches," I say. "You made them, remember? You cut them into cat shapes."

She rubs her eyes. "Did I?"

"Yes. You cut out the bread shapes and I ate the crusts for breakfast."

She nods. "And did you have lunch?"

I don't answer. It's one of those situations where you think is it worth saying this thing or will it just make life more complicated? I guess it's a bit like Miss Sharma and Mason's ice cream. It was just easier for her to let him finish the ice cream outside than have to sort it out.

"Why don't you have a bit more sleep?" I say.

She closes her eyes and I tiptoe out. Thomas follows me into the kitchen. Two potatoes wrapped in foil sit in the fruit bowl. I put the oven on.

Thomas keeps meowing and rubbing against my legs. I think I prefer him when he ignores me. Then I notice his bowl's full of cornflakes. He might not have minded if there'd been milk in there too but the cornflakes are dry. I tip them into the bin, fill the bowl with cat food and he's happy. So happy, in fact, that he completely ignores me. We're back to normal.

Girl in the film

I don't tell Mimi about the girl in the film because it doesn't make sense and she gets confused anyway, but I do tell her about the old cameras I saw and she tries to explain how they worked (it's complicated). It's all about light and shadows and lenses and film and magic paper.

I tell the seagull about the girl in the film, though (telepathically in case Mason hears), and she tilts her head and gives me a look as if to say *Life can be strange*.

When I try to sleep the girl goes round and round in my head. She's smiling at me and waving. It's confusing. She's got red hair like Mum but she's too old to be Mum and her hair's the wrong colour for Mimi. But whoever she is she stays with me all night, filling my dreams.

Notes for Mimi

9. *The girl staying with you is called Iris. Rena is Iris's mum and she's grown up now. Rena hasn't worn school uniform for twenty-five years because she hasn't been to school for twenty-five years.*
10. *If you made Iris sandwiches for lunch, it means Iris had sandwiches for lunch.*
11. *Cats don't like cornflakes, especially without milk.*

Note for me

2. *Don't trust Mason. He's greedy.*

7
DOGS

Lola and Bonnie are rescue dogs.

Lola's got long sandy hair that hangs over her eyes and ears and her pink tongue's always sticking out. When she first moved in with Lee and Danny she was so nervous she kept curling into a ball to make herself invisible. (It didn't work. She's big.) But now she's the happiest dog you could ever see. She pads around with her long hair blowing in the wind like an advert for dog shampoo.

Bonnie is completely the opposite. She's small and brown and black and white and she's got a sweet little face and shiny brown eyes. She's got short hair and little twitching ears and her tail always swings from side to side as if she's a clockwork toy and someone's wound her up.

And Bonnie really loves Lola. She always showing off and trying to get her attention. And when it rains she stands underneath Lola, even though water streams down Lola's coat and Bonnie gets wetter and wetter. But Bonnie doesn't mind. I think she feels safe.

But the funny thing is (and this is my bad luck) Lola and Bonnie are two of the nicest animals in the world and they live right opposite one of the meanest animals in the world (Thomas). Because Thomas is the least friendly cat you could ever meet. When I moved in he kept sitting outside my bedroom meowing and scratching at the door. (I think he wanted the bed back.) And now he ignores me completely. Like if it was just me living with Thomas I'd think I didn't exist.

And Thomas is especially horrible to Lola and Bonnie. One time Lee got locked out of his house and he came round because Mimi keeps his spare keys. And while Mimi was looking for them, Thomas stood in the kitchen doorway and arched his back and hissed at Lola and Bonnie, like he was saying *Don't you dare come any closer*. And the funny thing was Lola just shrugged and stretched out on the hall floor and Bonnie hid behind her, her little ears twitching. Because Thomas looked quite scary. If he did that in my bedroom, he could have the bed back and I'd be sleeping in his basket. (Luckily he doesn't know that.)

Anyway, Mimi spent forever searching for the keys and the dogs waited in the hall and Lee sat at the kitchen table in his little pool of stillness and I waited too.

"Sorry about this," I said.

It was a bit embarrassing.

Lee smiled. "No problem," he said. "Where else would I be?"

I wasn't sure what he meant so I made him a cup of tea and then I said, "What do you mean by *where else would I be?*"

"Well," he said, "where would I rather be than here? This is a fine place to be."

And he certainly didn't look like he minded waiting. He looked like he wouldn't mind at all if the world stopped unexpectedly for a few hours (or even forever).

And when Mimi came downstairs she ran into the kitchen and said, "Did I hear the kettle boil?" And she'd forgotten about the keys.

But when I gave Lee a look he said, "Not to worry, Danny will be home from work soon. No rush."

And he just waited and he told us funny stories about the dogs. And then he showed us some yoga in the living room and Mimi fell over because the space between the sofa and Thomas's basket was too small. And it was really funny. And I was glad Lee was having to wait for Danny and I wasn't even sure why I had minded in the first place because none of us were in a hurry anyway.

And when Danny came to collect Lee, Mimi said, "Well, that was a lovely surprise. You must come for tea more often."

And no one said a word about what a strange thing it was for her to say. No one even pulled a face. And as soon as Lola and Bonnie saw Danny they jumped all over him and couldn't wait to get out of the front door.

Stuff

The sun's glinting through the kitchen window. Thomas is asleep on a kitchen chair in a little pool of sunlight. The seagull's calling from the top of the shed.

Mimi's tidying. I'm sitting at the table eating toast and honey while she holds up tea towels one at a time. If I like a tea towel, I nod, and Mimi puts it back in the drawer. If I shake my head, they go in a bag to give away.

I want her to keep the one with the puppies on and the one with the dinosaur driving a spaceship, but I don't want the ones with recipes on (boring).

Mimi must have about a million tea towels. The bag's nearly full but she's still got loads left.

"Why do you have so many?" I say. "Do you like washing up?"

She laughs. "Not especially," she says. "I've got too much of everything." Her glasses are sliding down her nose.

"When I was a child I had very little," she says, "and since then I've never liked throwing things away."

"What was your childhood like?" I say.

"Well," Mimi says, "I don't remember my father, but my mother had lots of jobs, I do remember that. My favourite was when she worked as a waitress in the Ocean Restaurant on the West Pier. I used to play there after school. The kitchen staff would give me chips, the anglers at the end of the pier would give me mackerel, and the fortune teller would pretend to tell my fortune."

"How did you know she was pretending?"

"Because she always told me something different. Sometimes she said that I'd have five children, other times I'd live with twenty cats, sometimes she'd say I'd spend my life on a farm, other times I'd be a sailor. I think

it was a nice break for her not having to be too serious."
She laughs. "And funnily enough I believed everything
she told me. I thought everything was possible."

She takes an eggcup off the shelf and peers at it through
her glasses. Then she drops it in the bag.

"One minute," she says, "I'll show you something."

She hurries out of the kitchen and comes back a few
minutes later with a black-and-white photo. A laughing
woman wearing an apron and frilly hat is standing next
to a little out-of-focus jumping girl.

"Me and my mother," says Mimi, "in the restaurant
on the West Pier."

Mimi's mother looks like her and not like her but
together they look perfect. For some reason I want to hug
Mimi really tight. So I do. Her glasses fall off her nose.
Outside the seagull calls twelve times – *kee-yah kee-yah*
kee-yah kee-yah kee-yah kee-yah kee-yah kee-yah kee-yah
kee-yah kee-yah kee-yah.

Litter picking

Mason's taking his role as Eco Rep very seriously. He's
set up a playground tidy rota and he's trying to stop
everyone bringing plastic bottles into school. And now
he's going litter picking on the beach. And even though

he's really quite annoying (and a bit embarrassing) I'm going too.

He's so excited he runs all the way to the seafront, which means I have to run as well. As we wait at the traffic lights he's jumping from foot to foot. We've got gardening gloves and a black bag each and he's got his gloves on already and is waving his bag around.

"I wonder what we'll find," he says.

"Rubbish?" I say.

"Yes, but what sort of rubbish? And what else? We could find treasure, like gold washed up on the beach."

"Really?" I say. "Do you really think that?"

He shrugs. "Maybe."

I realise we're expecting completely different things. I think we'll find plastic bottles and old cans and crisp packets and Mason thinks he might get rich.

When the lights change we run across the road, down the slope and on to the beach. It's misty and the sea and sky merge into grey. The wind farm's disappeared completely. The beach is almost empty apart from a few people in hats and coats looking at the sea or sitting on plastic chairs outside the cafés. Seagulls settle on the West Pier.

Mason's like a dog looking for a bone. He races off across the stones, grabbing litter and stuffing it into his bag. Three seagulls fly around above him, trying to work out what he's doing. He must be confusing from above. He grabs a paper bag from a woman sitting at a table and a chip falls out.

"Oi!" she shouts.

"Sorry," says Mason, and keeps on running.

We find plastic bags and bottles, paper cups, plastic lids, beer tins, sweet wrappers, a toothbrush, a pen, bits of old newspapers, a toy dinosaur and a broken comb, all waiting to choke the seagulls or to be carried out to sea and eaten by fish.

"Right," says Mason. "Chips."

False teeth

The deckchair woman lets us sit on the deckchairs. They're not that comfortable but it feels like a treat. We've each got a bag of chips and we're holding them tight so the seagulls can't grab them. Little drops of rain are plopping on to the stones.

"Do you know your grandma talks to the moon?" says Mason.

"No she doesn't."

He smirks.

"She does," he says. "I've seen her."

(Every time I think he might be OK he reminds me how annoying he is.)

"I don't believe you," I say.

He shrugs. Then he takes a chip, throws it into the air and catches it in his mouth. He's such a show-off. I pretend I didn't see.

"Did I tell you about my grandad losing his teeth?" he says.

I shake my head.

"Well," he says, "he was sitting in Angie's garden behind her shop in his shorts and vest."

"Why?"

"Because it was summer, duh. And he put his teeth on the table next to his cup of tea."

"You mean they're false teeth?"

"Yes, they all come out. Top and bottom. Do you want to know what happened or not?"

I shrug. (I'm not sure I do.)

"Anyway," he says, "he was having a little sleep and a seagull stole his teeth."

"No!" I say.

"The seagull flew right off towards the sea with the teeth in its beak. He never got them back."

He starts to laugh and then he chokes on a chip.

His eyes look like they're going to pop out of his head. I thump him between the shoulder blades. I really (honestly truly) don't want to have to do the Heimlich manoeuvre on Mason. The chip shoots out of his mouth. A seagull swoops down and flies off with it.

We're both laughing now. We can't stop. I'm hoping the deckchairs don't collapse.

"I thought," says Mason when he can finally breathe, "that I might find his teeth on the beach."

"Idiot," I say.

We keep laughing but there's something about Mason's grandad in his shorts and vest watching a seagull fly away with his teeth that also makes me feel bad. And I can tell by Mason's face he feels the same.

Smiley face

I don't realise how cold I am until I get home. I really want a shower but a cold shower would be horrible so I do without. (You could say I'm keeping away from all water.)

I text Dad.

Can you fix Mimi's shower? Or I might never wash again.

He replies with a smiley face. He's probably waiting

for Mum to get home so he can sort out the damp in my bedroom. Or maybe he's trying to get the twins to have a bath. A hot bath.

8
TORNADO

My mum likes to be organised, which might be why living in a house that's falling apart makes her so grumpy. She's a doctor in a hospital so she's got lots of lives to save, which is probably why she can never relax. But even when she's home her head's full of jobs and any time she opens her mouth they just pop out. She's the most stressful person in the world.

I don't even know why she tells me to daydream. You could never daydream when she's around. You honestly can't. It's impossible to even be with her without her giving you an instruction or asking a question. It usually takes about ten seconds but never more than a minute. Sometimes all I need to do is catch her eye.

"Have you done your homework?"

"When's parents' evening?"

"Where's your sock?"

"I've put a rubber in your pencil case in case you need it." (I've already got two.)

"We need to get you to the dentist." (A month after my last appointment when my teeth were fine.)

It's like having a tornado fizzing round my head.

Dad says the house is falling down from the outside but I think it's falling down from the inside too. He blames the weather but I blame the people inside. Too much noise and worry. Too much of everything all mixed up with the wind and the rain crashing in. The house probably wants to collapse into a heap and forget about everything (I know I do sometimes).

In the summer it all got too much for Mum and she packed a case and said, "I'm moving in with Mimi." And she walked out of the door, leaving Dad and me with our mouths so wide open a whole swarm of flies could have flown in.

"Hey ho," said Dad. "Better get tea on."

He looked like a cartoon character who'd been hit by a

plank, like there should be little stars dancing around his head. He had to make tea because we were hungry, but I think he would have preferred to play statues with the twins or crawl under the table and stay there for at least a week. It was awkward.

I rolled my eyes like I do when Dad forgets to do up his fly or gets all complicated and bossy in the kitchen when he only has an egg to fry. Pearl and Noah did the same, only they can't quite roll their eyes. They did a funny head-bobbing thing instead.

Anyway, Mum stayed at Mimi's for one night and then came home. Four weeks later I moved in.

Swirling sea

Me and Mason are back at the flea market. Mason's running around and jiggling his money. I'm looking at the stalls.

"What do you think?" he says. He holds a marble up to the sky. "Don't you think it looks like a ship on a swirling sea?"

It does. The sea's sort of swirling green and the sky's grey and there's a little dark shape like a boat in the middle tangled with the sea.

"It's a whole world in there," he says. "That's why I

like them so much."

I nod. A bit bored really. I mostly came because I want to go to the sweet shop.

"It's called a tornado by the way," says Mason.

I nod again. Then I notice his wrist. My heart does its little scream.

"What's that?" I say.

"This?" says Mason.

He waves his hand and a bracelet slides down his arm. It's got red wooden beads, metal beads and a green tin whistle on a bit of string.

"It's for my mum," he says.

I'm trying to stop myself exploding.

"It's Mimi's," I say, "and you know it. You took it from Mimi's house."

"I don't know what you're talking about," he says. "I got it with the marble."

"Give it to me!" I say.

I try to snatch it but he puts his arm behind his back.

"It's mine," Mason says. "I bought it over there. It was two things for 50p so I got it for my mum."

He points at a woman standing behind a stall wearing a hat with a feather in it. She gives us a little wave.

"I've never even been in your grandma's house," he says, "except the kitchen, because you never invite me in. Because you're waiting for secondary school to find a friend, and spending time with me is just until you find someone better."

He sounds so upset a little voice in my head is wondering if he might be telling the truth.

"The thing is," I say, "there isn't another bracelet. Mimi's dad made it for her. There aren't any more." My voice is cracking.

"Well, she shouldn't have got rid of it then, should she?" says Mason. "If it's so special."

Mimi getting rid of the bracelet is an awful thought. I don't know what to say. Either Mason's lying or Mimi gave away her most precious thing. And both of those things are terrible.

Mason pulls the bracelet off his wrist and hands it to me. "My mum wouldn't want it anyway," he says. "It's rubbish. I only got it because there wasn't anything else."

"I'll pay you back."

He shrugs. "You know," he says, "you're really horrible. I think you're probably the most horrible person I've ever met."

And he walks away. And as he does I know he didn't steal the bracelet and I feel really, really awful.

Feet tapping

We don't go to the sweet shop. We go home. Everything's spoilt. Mason marches on ahead and I hurry after him. I'm trying not to step on the cracks but it's not easy when I'm rushing. The bracelet jangles against my wrist.

"Do you think I should tell Mimi where we found it?" I say.

I imagine Mimi searching for the bracelet, her feet tap-tapping up the stairs, her head spinning.

"Maybe she didn't want it," he says. "Maybe that's why she gave it away."

"Of course she wanted it. It's her favourite thing."

"Well, she does do strange things," he says. "Like my grandad."

I think of his grandad in his shorts and vest watching as the seagull flies off with his teeth and I feel really annoyed.

"She's nothing like your grandad."

"How do you know? You've never met him. And you never will. And you're never coming to the Sweet Suite again either."

"I don't want to anyway," I say, "because you're such a show-off. And if you don't mind me saying –" I know he'll mind me saying – "you probably shouldn't show your teeth to customers, even if you don't have any fillings. It puts them right off."

Mason looks so upset I wish I'd not said anything. He walks ahead of me and I imagine his face squeezed tight.

The rest of the way back he won't speak. And I try really hard not to say anything nasty or even to think anything nasty.

"Thank you for finding the bracelet," I say when we get home. "Mimi will be so happy."

"Whatever," he says. His face is hot and sad.

He goes into his house and shuts the door behind him. I feel terrible. I've got Mimi's bracelet that she gave away and I've been horrible to my only friend. Because I suppose Mason is a friend. Sort of.

A million creases

Mimi's in the kitchen peeling potatoes. I hold out my wrist and a cloud crosses her face.

"I'd really rather you didn't take that out," she says.

"I didn't," I say. "Mason found it at the flea market. He bought it for 50p."

Her face falls into a million creases. She drops a potato into a pan and puts her hands to her face.

"Are you saying I threw it out?"

I shrug really gently so she can pretend not to see. Then I take off the bracelet and give it to her. She carries it into the living room, cupping it in her hands like it's an unhatched egg. Then she screams.

"Iris!"

I run in after her. She's standing by the mantelpiece, a bracelet in each hand. Her head's wobbling.

"Look!" she says. "Two bracelets!"

I take them from her and as soon as I do I honestly don't know which is which. They've both got five red wooden beads, three metal beads and a green whistle on a bit of string.

"How can there be two?" I say. "I don't understand."

Mimi shakes her head. "I don't know."

We hold the bracelets up to the window and turn them in our hands to see if we can find a difference. And then we do – the new bracelet has a *CB* carved into a wooden bead.

"It's Coral's!" Mimi shrieks. "Coral Butterworth! My father must have made them after Coral was born. This is hers!"

I look at the photo on the mantelpiece and peer at the little girl's hand to see if she's wearing the bracelet but the photo's too small to tell. Mimi can't tell either so I put on her glasses and try again. You might think her glasses would give me super-strong vision but it doesn't work like that. I get an instant headache. Everything's out of focus.

"Never mind," says Mimi. "What matters is the bracelets are both here!"

She does a little dance and so do I. I'm so happy Mimi didn't throw the bracelet out. She's not like Mason's grandad at all. She's absolutely fine.

"Right," says Mimi, "show me where you got it."

Happy

We skip out of the house like two five-year-olds. Yes, it's embarrassing, and, yes, when we get to the end of the street I stop, but for a few moments I don't care. We're wearing a bracelet each and they rattle against our wrists. The seagull's happy too. She calls twelve times from the roof then flies down the road ahead of us.

The market's closing. It's beginning to spit with rain. The woman with the feather in her hat is loading stuff into a van.

"Excuse me," Mimi says, "do you remember where you got this?" She holds out her wrist.

"Oh," says the woman, "that funny little bracelet. Yes, a boy bought it from me earlier. It came in a box of bits."

"We've got two," I say, holding out mine.

"Very nice," says the woman.

She's not that interested. She wants to put her stuff away.

"Where did you get it?" says Mimi.

"No idea. An auction maybe or a house clearance or a charity shop. Or sometimes people bring me things."

"Could we see the box?" Mimi says.

"If you must, darling," says the woman. "Hang on."

She digs around under her table and comes up holding a small battered cardboard box with a torn label.

"Just a few bits in here," she says. "I was going to put them out next time."

"Can I buy the box?" says Mimi.

"Of course," says the woman. "One pound and it's yours. Do you want to look inside?"

Mimi shakes her head. The rain's getting heavier. She hands over £1. Slowly. She does that embarrassing thing where she gets out all the coins one by one and puts them in the woman's hand. The stallholder doesn't seem to mind. Mimi probably took her wedding photos.

I want to look in the box right now but Mimi wants to get home. She carries it close to her chest, hunching over it to keep it dry, and I imagine all the things that might be in there – photos of Coral perhaps and letters

96

and toys. I'm so excited I keep running ahead and then having to wait for Mimi to catch up.

When we open the front door Thomas comes running down the hall and rubs himself against Mimi's legs.

"Whose cat is this?" she says, shaking him off.

I pretend I didn't hear.

Fishing boat

Here's what we find in the box:

Six little bags with old-fashioned wooden kits inside for making model planes.

A little wooden fishing boat with faded red paint and frayed bits of string hung from the sails.

And that's it. There are no photos or letters or toys. It's a bit disappointing.

"Why do you think Coral's bracelet was in there?" I say.

"I've no idea," says Mimi, "but how wonderful that I've got it now. You must thank your friend."

"I wasn't very nice to him actually," I say. "I thought he'd stolen it from you."

Mimi raises her eyebrows. "I wonder he puts up with you," she says. "Really I do."

I feel ashamed.

"Can we make him a cake and invite him round?" I say. "And give him his 50p back?"

"Good idea," Mimi says. "We can give him the plane kits too and the fishing boat. Unless you'd like them."

"I'd like some of the plane kits," I say. "But Mason can have some too and he can have the fishing boat."

"OK," says Mimi.

I have a trick

I have a trick. It's very useful for school or family or friends. Any situation really. What it is, is I can make myself look one way when I feel another way inside. So I can raise one eyebrow like I'm a scientist trying to solve a problem when actually I'm wondering what's for pudding and I can look like I'm fascinated by the twins' games when I'm just wishing they'd go to bed. My dad knows I do it. I'm not sure Mum's ever noticed.

And now I can smile at Mimi and pretend everything's fine when really it feels like the opposite.

Because I've been horrible to Mason and I'm going to have to let him in the house and show him the bracelets. And I know he'll take his time and look at everything and touch everything. And he'll probably want to talk about his grandad too. And I really don't want to

98

talk about his grandad ever again.

And I can't understand why Coral's bracelet was in the box with the model kits. Mimi says it doesn't matter but it matters to me. Because things don't just end up places for no reason.

And Mimi didn't recognise Thomas and that's really scary. Because Thomas looked exactly the same as usual.

The seagull's calling from the roof – twelve times. Maybe she's telling me things will be better when I'm twelve or maybe there are twelve things we need to find out about Coral or maybe Mason will touch twelve things when he comes round tomorrow (or break twelve things even). Or maybe the cat wasn't Thomas at all but was an identical cat (like me and the girl in the film). And the seagull's telling me there are twelve cats identical to Thomas somewhere out in the world.

Notes for Mimi
12. *Be careful what you give away. Make sure it's nothing you really want to keep.*
13. *The black-and-white cat in the house is your cat. He's called Thomas.*

Note for me
3. *Stop being horrible to Mason.*

9
ROBOTS

If you've never had mould in your room, you might not be able to imagine it, but if you think of an alien breaking in through the walls that's what it's like. And there's nothing good about it. It's just horrible. It rubs on your clothes and spreads across the walls like a shadow. And if you breathe it in, it's bad for you. I know all this because that's why I ended up sleeping on the floor in the twins' room.

And now there's scaffolding outside my mouldy bedroom. And whenever Dad gets a minute, like when

Mum's back from work or the twins are asleep, he climbs up the scaffold and squeezes stuff into the holes between the bricks. To stop the rain getting in. And (I'm pleased to say) it's taking ages. I'm hoping he won't finish it until the twins start school or better still have grown up.

And if you don't know what it's like to share a room with two-year-old twins, imagine two robots that haven't been programmed properly and no one knows how to switch them off. So one moment they're jumping up and down and a minute later they're screaming and a minute after that they're angry because their beds are too hot or too cold. Or their cover keeps slipping off the bed or their sheets are not smooth enough or the sheets are too smooth or too itchy or not itchy enough. Or they're not tired or they're too tired. Or there's too much light coming in through the curtains or there's not enough light. And, worst of all, sometimes they want opposite things! (Argh!)

And that's why I ended up moving in with Mimi.

Peas

We're making a chocolate cake for Mason. Mimi's weighing the ingredients and I'm mixing them together. Mimi's wearing her apron with the yellow ribbons sewn on to the pockets and she's doing a little dance. It's all going well until she tips frozen peas into the eggs. Little green balls sink into the yellow.

"Isn't it pretty?" she says.

It's confusing. One moment I'm beating eggs for a cake, the next I'm making an omelette.

"Do we want frozen peas?" I say.

Mimi nods.

"Of course. Why ever not?"

"Because we're making chocolate cake," I say, "and you don't usually put peas in a chocolate cake."

"Oh," she says.

It takes ages to fish out the peas and all the time Mimi doesn't say a word.

Not bothered

Mason's in his garden poking at things with a stick.

I shout to him through the hedge. "Mason, do you want some cake?"

He doesn't answer.

The seagull's standing on the shed. She tilts her head and looks at me. (She'd probably like some cake.)

"Please, Mason," I say, "come and have some cake! Me and Mimi made it to say thank you."

"No thanks."

"It's chocolate cake," I say.

"Not bothered," he says.

He does sound a bit bothered.

I crouch down next to the hedge. "I'm sorry about yesterday," I say. "Sorry I was annoying."

His face appears through the hole. "You were more than annoying," he says. "You were horrible."

He crawls through the gap, stands up and shakes himself down. His glasses are lopsided.

"I get a bit fed up of you always being so nasty," he says. "I don't even know why you're like that." He takes a deep breath. "Why are you like that?"

I shrug. "I don't know," I say. "I'm sorry."

(Actually I don't know.)

"Well," he says, "I hope Mimi was happy to get her bracelet back. Maybe she should be more careful next time."

"She was happy," I say, "only it wasn't her bracelet. It was Coral's."

"What do you mean?"

"Coral, Mimi's cousin. The girl who drowned. It was her bracelet. Mimi's dad made one for Mimi and one for Coral. Mimi's has *MB* carved on it for Mimi Butterworth, and Coral's has *CB* on it for Coral Butterworth."

Mason frowns. "Wow," he says. "Do you think it came from the bottom of the sea and the tide brought it in?"

"Maybe," I say. "Or maybe the sea monster burped it up."

"What sea monster?"

"The one that ate Coral."

(The words pop out. I can't stop them.)

"What are you talking about?"

It's embarrassing. You know that feeling when something you think is a perfectly ordinary way of thinking pops out and you realise it's not other people's way of thinking? It's awkward. I clear my throat and try to sound like a teacher giving assembly.

"I just have a theory," I say, "that maybe a sea monster tipped over the boat and ate Coral and her parents."

Mason rolls his eyes. "Duh," he says.

"It's just a theory," I say. "It's probably not true."

(I know it is.)

He doesn't say a word but I can tell he thinks I'm completely weird.

"Anyway," I say, "we made a cake to say thank you. And we're going to give you your 50p back. And we went back to the market and the woman said it came from a box that had model plane kits in and we're going to give you some of the model kits. And there was a little fishing boat and you can have that too."

"Really?" says Mason.

He's gone from not interested to jumping up and down. His eyes are shining.

"OK," he says.

He looks like he's about to run into the house, like if I hadn't invited him he'd be in there anyway.

Catch

Mimi's kneeling on the living-room floor sorting through a drawer of old video cassettes.

"Hello," she says to Mason. "And who might you be?"

"Mason," says Mason.

He gives me a look and then gives everything else a look. And I mean everything. His eyes are nearly dropping out of his head.

"All this stuff," he says. "Wow!"

Mimi looks pleased.

Mason looks at every single thing on the walls and the shelves, picking them up and putting them down again. Then he sees the bracelets.

"I don't think my mum would want one of these

anyway," he says. "They're a bit plain."

He puts one on each wrist and starts to punch the air.

Mimi doesn't look pleased any more. She looks as though she's waiting for him to throw the bracelets across the room and she has to be ready to catch them.

What I've realised about Mason is he doesn't know when to stop. I think that's why he's so annoying. It's like he'll pick anything up, even if it's not his, and say things about Mimi I don't want to hear and that aren't even true.

"Can you put them back?" I say.

I'm trying not to sound too annoyed.

He shrugs, takes them off and puts them on the mantelpiece.

Mimi looks relieved. She closes the drawer and goes into the kitchen.

Mason picks up the photo of Coral. "Who's this?" he says.

"That's Coral. It was her bracelet."

"Is she wearing it?" he says.

I shrug. "Don't know."

He peers at it through his glasses but he can't tell either. The photo's too small.

Feeding seagulls

We're eating chocolate cake. Mason's put the box on the kitchen table and taken everything out and laid it in a row next to the 50p Mimi gave him. It's lucky I've taken my plane kits upstairs or he'd want to lay them out too and there's hardly enough room for our plates.

"I'm going to make a plane first," he says, "and then I'm going to paint the boat and fix the strings so it looks brand new."

He thinks it's his birthday.

"Thank you so much for finding the bracelet, Malcolm," says Mimi. "What a kind boy you are."

Mason beams. "You're welcome," he says.

He doesn't mind she's got his name wrong again. He wants more cake.

"Would you like another slice?" says Mimi.

"Yes please," says Mason.

"Not you, though," says Mimi. She's looking at me. "You need to get back to your job. Those seagulls need feeding."

Mason's eyes swivel from me to Mimi and back again. I'm hoping he's not going to snort. He does. I kick him under the table. Then we all freeze. It's like we're in a film and it's stopped and nobody knows how to get it started again.

At last I say, "Mimi, I'm Iris. I don't have a job. I'm still at school."

(I'm trying to imagine what the job would be feeding seagulls.)

"She's ten," says Mason (un)helpfully.

Mimi shakes her head as if there's an insect stuck in her hair. (There isn't.)

Then she says, "I do know that. I don't always need to be told the obvious."

And she gets up and walks out of the kitchen. When we hear her go upstairs Mason gives another little snort and then, because I don't laugh, he looks at me with sad eyes.

"Uh-oh," he says.

Mason being sorry for me is even worse than him thinking Mimi's weird.

I shrug. I don't understand what happened but I hate that Mason saw it and now he's giving me sad eyes. I don't say a word until eventually he puts his things back in the box and gets up to go.

"You won't tell anyone, will you?" I say. "That Mimi got a bit muddled."

He shakes his head. I'm hoping he's not going to say anything about his grandad. He doesn't.

Instead he says, "Can I take some cake?"

"Yes," I say, "and can I come back to the Sweet Suite sometime?"

He nods. Then he cuts himself a (massive) slice of cake, puts it in the box, carries it into the garden and crawls back through the hedge.

Dressing gown

Mimi's flying up into the night sky. Her arms are outstretched and she's wearing her dressing gown and slippers. I'm watching her get further and further away and trying to call her back. From somewhere in the distance I hear knocking. I shudder awake. I'm in bed. Someone's tapping on the window. My heart's racing.

"Iris!"

It's Mason.

I jump out of bed and pull back the curtains. He's standing on the flat roof outside my room, his face pressed to the glass. I open the window and he leans in. He's wearing a jumper over his pyjamas and waving the box and a torch.

"What are you doing?" I say. "You gave me a fright!"

"Come out!" he says. "I've got something to show you."

I hesitate.

"Come on," he says, "it's important!"

His head's bobbing up and down.

I pull on a jumper and climb out of the window. It's cold but the sky's full of stars. The moon lights up the rooftops. Mason's actually got himself a cushion. He sits on it, adjusts his glasses and shines his torch on the box. I sit next to him on the hard, cold roof.

But just as he's about to show me whatever it is, the kitchen door opens below us and Mimi walks into the garden. She's wearing her dressing gown and slippers.

"Good evening, beautiful moon," she says.

Mason squeals.

Mimi looks round to see where the noise comes from. She can't see us. She probably thinks it's the seagull. A horrible whistle is coming out of Mason.

"I told you," he mouths. "She talks to the moon."

"Lovely moon," says Mimi again. "Good to see you as always."

It's so embarrassing. I drop my head into my hands and Mason does the same, only I'm hiding and he's sniggering. I glare at him between my fingers. I wonder if he'll ever stop.

Mimi spends ages talking to the moon while the cold wraps round us. She tells the moon about Coral's bracelet and the beach and our seagull and Lola and Bonnie and how she's having a big tidy. Mason stops laughing. He's fed up. He wants to go back inside.

Eventually Mimi wanders back into the house.

Mason jumps up. "The address on the box is Angie's shop," he hisses. "It's the address of the Sweet Suite!"

"What?"

"It's Angie's address," he says.

He picks up his cushion, walks over to his window and shoves it into his room with the box and torch.

"I thought you might want to know. It's just a pity I had to nearly freeze to death to tell you."

Then he climbs through his window and pulls it shut behind him.

Asleep on the sofa

It doesn't make sense. Why was Coral's bracelet in a box with Angie's address on? I'm pacing up and down my room trying to work it out but I can't. I go downstairs. I want to look at the bracelets again.

I creep into the living room as quietly as I can. I don't want Thomas waking up and running upstairs and stealing my bed. He's asleep on the sofa for a change. Not in his basket. He looks like he's about to slide on to the floor.

The moon shines in through the gap in the curtains, glinting on the bracelets. I put one on each wrist and clasp my hands together as if I'm saying a little prayer. Which I sort of am. I'm wishing and wishing for something. Something to make everything make sense.

When Thomas stretches and yawns I take the bracelets off, put them back on the mantelpiece and tiptoe back to bed. And then I sleep.

Notes for Mimi

14. *Don't put peas in chocolate cake. Carrots go in cakes sometimes but not peas.*

15. *Iris is ten years old and she doesn't have a job. She goes to school.*

16. *Iris doesn't feed the seagulls either. The seagulls feed themselves.*

17. *The boy next door is called Mason. Though if you give him cake and model kits he won't mind what you call him.*

10
CLEAN WASHING

Mimi's sorting through a pile of clean washing when I come down for breakfast.

"Did you do this?" she says.

She shakes out a T-shirt. Small hairs drift to the floor.

"Do what?" I say.

"Put the clean washing in Thomas's basket."

"No."

She folds the T-shirt. Not happy. Not smiling.

It's only when I set off for school that I remember Thomas sleeping on the sofa last night. Now it makes

113

sense. (Sort of.)

Across to France

Mason's carrying the cardboard box like it's the most precious thing in the world. We're going to show Angie after school. He's made one of the model planes. He said it was easy.

Every few minutes he takes the plane out of the box and throws it into the air. It flies pretty well, if I'm honest. I'm going to make mine. And when Mason's not flying the plane or running after it we try to imagine why Coral's bracelet was in the box with Angie's address on it.

Here's what we think.

Mason thinks a tourist found the bracelet on the beach and gave it to his children who swapped it for sweets from the Sweet Suite.

I think Coral lived in the flat above Angie's shop and used to make model planes, and years later someone found the planes and the bracelet and put them in the box.

Then we think a seagull pulled the bracelet off Coral's wrist and flew across the sea to France with it and it took years for the sea to carry it back to Brighton. This is Mason's idea. (Of course. He's hoping the same will happen with his grandad's teeth.)

And finally we think maybe Angie is Coral's long-lost relative. Which means me and Mason are long-lost relatives. (This is a bit shocking for both of us.)

Working hard or hardly working

We're doing long division in class. Well, trying to. Mason keeps nudging me and smirking. He's got the box under his desk and every few minutes he looks down to check it's still there.

He passes me a bit of paper with a fish drawn on it. Underneath he's written *Maybe the bracelet was swallowed by a fish!!!* I put a smiley face on it and pass it back.

"Iris," says Miss Sharma, "do you have anything you'd like to share with the class?"

I'm confused. It's like I've come up from deep water and I can't quite focus on land.

"No, miss," I say.

She raises her eyebrows. "How about you, Mason? Working hard or hardly working?"

"What?" says Mason.

"Are you working hard or hardly working?"

"Hardly working," he says.

Miss Sharma raises her eyebrows.

"But I am enjoying your class."

(Yes, honestly he says that. If he was smirking, it might be funny but he's not. He looks deadly serious. The rest of the class is smirking.)

"Good," says Miss Sharma. "You won't mind extending the lesson into break then, will you?"

"No," says Mason, "I'd like that."

(It's as though someone else is making his mouth work.)

"You too, Iris," says Miss Sharma. "You can practise your long division during break and you can finish your conversation on your way home."

Many moons

The day lasts forever. When the bell finally goes we run out of the playground, tripping over little kids waiting for their parents. Three seagulls squabble at the gate. Someone's dropped a sandwich, which lies open on the pavement.

"Cheese and pickle," says Mason. "Yuck."

The seagulls don't think it's yuck. They're tearing it apart.

We run all the way to the Sweet Suite and crash into the shop. (Well, Mason does. I follow.)

"Hi, Mason and not-Mason's-friend," says Angie.

Mason puts the box on to the counter and opens the lid.

"Where did you get that?" says Angie.

"The flea market," says Mason. "It's got this address on."

"I know," she says. "I found it at the back of the attic. I put some things on the doorstep for people to help themselves to. I should have kept the model kits for you, shouldn't I? Sorry about that."

"That's OK," says Mason.

"There was a bracelet in there," I say. "It belonged to my grandma."

It's not quite true but I get the impression Angie wouldn't like a full explanation. Customers are wandering around the shop, looking at the shelves of sweets. A woman's fixing her lipstick in front of the mirrors.

"Interesting," says Angie (sounding not very interested).

The lipstick woman's combing her hair now.

Angie looks impatient. "If you don't mind," she says, "I really have to get on."

"Can we help?" says Mason.

"No thanks," says Angie.

Mason shrugs. Then, for no reason that I can understand, he takes the model plane out of the box and throws it across the shop. It lands high on a shelf behind a jar of flying saucers. Everyone looks round.

"Mason," says Angie, "for goodness' sake."

She stands on a little stool, rescues the plane and puts it back in the box. Then she puts two sherbet lemons in a paper bag, hands them to Mason and says, "Not that you deserve these. Now off you go. One each."

We walk home in silence. Partly because Coral's bracelet is still a mystery and partly because we're sucking sherbet lemons.

Shower

Dad's fixing Mimi's shower. The house smells of baking. Mimi and the twins are lying on the living-room floor with their legs in the air. Like insects that need to be flicked over. I go upstairs to see Dad. He's standing in the bath doing something to the boiler.

"Hello, sweetheart," he says. "How are you doing?"

He clambers out and gives me a hug. He smells of soap and banana.

"I'm OK," I say.

"Just fixing this while Mimi keeps the twins occupied," he says, "then you can have a hot shower."

"Thanks, Dad," I say.

He smiles.

"You know Mimi's bracelet on her mantelpiece," I say, "the one from when she was a child?"

Dad nods.

"We found another one at the flea market. It belonged to Mimi's cousin. The one that drowned. It's exactly the same except it's got Coral's initials on it."

"Really?" says Dad. "How amazing!"

He's got something smeared on his jumper. It looks like egg.

"I'll show you when you come down," I say. "They're both on the mantelpiece now."

"OK," he says. "Oh, and by the way, the damp in your room's drying out well. You'll be able to come home soon."

"Will I?" I say.

"By Christmas for sure," he says. "You'll like that, won't you?"

I nod but I'm not sure. I've got to write notes for Mimi and I've got to solve the mystery of the bracelet. And anyway, I want to wait for the twins to grow up.

I leave Dad in the bathroom and run down the stairs. But before I've even reached the hall there's screaming.

Eggs

Mimi's standing in the kitchen wearing oven gloves and her apron with yellow ribbons. She's holding a cake tin in the air. Pearl and Noah are pulling at her sleeve.

"No!" she's shouting. "You can't have any. It's not right."

"We want some. We want some."

The tin is half full of what looks like a huge burnt biscuit.

"Did you put eggs in?" I say.

Mimi nods. "Of course. Eggs. Of course. You can't make cake without eggs, can you?" She wipes the back of her hand across her forehead. "Can you?"

I shake my head. "I don't think so."

Every surface is covered in ingredients. Sugar spills out of its bag, butter slides off its silver foil, flour is sprinkled on the kitchen floor. And a full box of eggs sits on the table.

"I think you forgot the eggs, Mimi," I say.

She shudders, then makes a dash for the bin and tries to shake out the cake/biscuit. Yellow crumbs fall to the floor, dry and horrible. Noah grabs a bit and shoves it into his mouth. He looks like he's eating sand. Dust sticks to his lips and cheeks.

"Don't eat it!" Mimi screams. "It'll make you sick!"

"That's rude," says Noah. "I want it! You said there'd be cake!"

I'm not going to tell you who says what next because I can't describe all the voices on top of each other. The twins are screaming, I can tell you that, and I'm trying to get them away and clear up the mess while Mimi makes chicken noises – angry chicken noises.

"What a fuss! What a fuss!"

She's almost clucking. I'm not kidding you.

And then Dad appears at the door. In my mind I'm the calm one scooping up the useless cake but when it's all sorted out he tells me I was screaming louder than anyone.

Big fat lie

"What's up, Iris?" says Dad.

Mimi's watching *Chitty Chitty Bang Bang* with the twins. They're eating the leftover chocolate cake (the bit Mason didn't take). Me and Dad are sitting at the kitchen table. All the surfaces are gleaming.

"Are you not happy here? Would you rather come home sooner?"

"No," I say. "I like it here."

"Then why so cross?"

I shrug. "The twins are quite annoying sometimes, aren't they?" I say.

"They can be hard work," he says. "That's why we thought you'd be happier here while we sort your room. But you can come home sooner if you prefer."

I shake my head. "I want to stay here. I like it."

"OK."

Dad, by the way, can see right into my brain. He can't tell what's going on in there but he can tell if something's hidden.

"Does Mimi do this sort of thing often?" he says. "Forget ingredients in recipes?"

"No." I'm shaking my head. "First time it's ever happened actually. Anything like that really. She doesn't forget things. In fact, she reminds me to do things."

I'm overdoing it a bit. It's a big fat lie and it's getting worse. I imagine the lie like a punch bag – I've just thwacked it as far as I can and it's about to swing back and hit me round the head.

Dad raises his eyebrows. "OK," he says.

I smile. A hard plastic smile I'm sure doesn't look right. I'm showing too many teeth but it's the best I can do.

"I was just disappointed about the cake," I say.

Dad opens his mouth to reply but before he can say another word Noah comes screaming into the kitchen.

"Mimi keeps playing the same bit!"

Pearl crashes in behind him and they stand together, their faces screwed up in anger.

"We don't want to see that bit any more."

"We want to see the flying car."

They're followed in by Mimi.

"I like that bit," says Mimi. "Why shouldn't I watch it again? It's my favourite bit."

"Which bit is it?" I say.

"'Truly Scrumptious'. The lovely song."

She begins to sing it in a soft high voice and for a moment it's quite sweet. But then the twins begin to scream and Dad starts jumping around, though not in a good way. It would be nice if he burst into song and we all sang "Truly Scrumptious" like the family in the film. But he doesn't. Instead he sort of explodes in slow motion. It's like he's got eight limbs instead of four and they're all moving in different directions.

"Right," he shouts. "Home!"

He wrestles the twins out of the house. I try to help but it makes things worse so me and Mimi stand back and watch. Mimi puts her hands over her ears and rolls her eyes. Dad kisses us goodbye and hurries away, his face like stone. We wave from the step.

When they've gone the house feels still and quiet. Seagulls squabble on Lee's roof but it's a nice sound.

Mimi spins round and gives me a kiss. "I've got an idea," she says. Her eyes are shining. "Let's make a cake."

I take a deep breath and pretend I didn't hear.

Flat and deflated

The shower works perfectly. It's lovely and warm. But when I go to bed I remember Dad forgot to look at the bracelets. And I feel quite bad. Because I think it's amazing we've got both the bracelets and Dad didn't even remember I told him.

I walk to the window and look out into the night. The seagull's standing on the flat roof staring up at me, her head to one side. I don't speak out loud but in my head I'm saying, *Dad didn't look at the bracelets.* The seagull doesn't make a sound either but she looks like she's thinking, *Never mind. That's grown-ups for you.*

I feel like the cake. Flat and deflated and full of the wrong ingredients. It takes me ages to fall asleep. I can't stop thinking about Coral and the mystery of the bracelet and Mimi getting so many things wrong. And how Coral should have been Mimi's friend for life. Not her imaginary friend.

Notes for Mimi

18. *Don't put clean washing in Thomas's basket. It'll get covered in cat hair.*
19. *If you don't put eggs in the cake, it will be dry and horrible and it will probably end up on the floor.*
20. *The twins don't like watching the same song in* Chitty Chitty Bang Bang *over and over. They get angry and then they cry.*
21. *If you've made cake already, don't make cake again the same day because everyone is a bit fed up with it.*

Note for me

4. *Find out what happened to Coral's bracelet.*

11
WEATHER

A funny thing about Mimi is sometimes her mood is like the weather. So if it's a stormy day she'll lose her temper easily. Scream even. Mum says she was always like that. One time when there was a storm and she was round at our house she picked up a mug and threw it. And nobody knew what she was angry about. Only she knew and as soon as the mug smashed it was like all her anger was gone and she couldn't remember what it was about in the first place. Mum had to walk out of the room. She was furious. She looked like she might explode.

"What was that all about?" Dad said when he'd cleared everything up.

Mimi's face crumpled. She looked like her thoughts were wading through mud.

"Such a shame," she said at last.

She looked down at Pearl, who was sitting on the floor pretending to read a newspaper. She wasn't being especially annoying.

"Is Pearl upsetting you?" said Dad.

"Such a shame," said Mimi.

"What's a shame?" I said.

Mimi shuddered. Her mouth wobbled and so did her head. Then she sighed. There was no anger left.

And when Dad went to find Mum and calm her down Mimi looked at me and smiled as though nothing was wrong at all. And until then I thought Mum was exaggerating. But when I saw the rainbow out of the window I thought maybe it was true.

And now I think something else might be true. Now I think maybe Mimi was talking about Coral.

Mason's marbles

Mason's crawled through the hedge carrying a tin. He knocks on the kitchen window and I let him in.

"Look, Iris," he says. "I want to show you my marbles."

He puts the tin on the kitchen table and takes off the lid.

"Shall I tell you the names of them all?"

"OK," I say.

I need to be nice to him after I've been so horrible.

We sit at the table and Mason gets out a little book and ticks off each of his marbles on a list.

"Why do you like marbles so much?"

"They're interesting."

"Are they?"

"Of course," he says. "Look at the colours."

He holds one up to the light and twists it in his fingers. It's white with a blue dolphin shape in the middle.

"And anyway," he says, "they remind me of my grandad. Because he told me the names. And now he can't always remember the names so I remember for him."

He looks sad and serious.

"And the names might be old-fashioned," he says, "but I like them."

"Well," I say, "they are interesting actually. It's probably just that I don't know enough about them."

Mason's face lights up. "I'll teach you!"

And that's the next hour gone while he tells me the names and I have to repeat them. It's not always a good idea to encourage an enthusiast. Not unless you've got loads of time. Mimi comes to sit with us, goes out and comes back again. Three times.

These are Mason's marbles:

12 tornados

10 galaxies

14 squids

16 oceans

68 cat's eyes

I have to admit they look beautiful. Boring but beautiful.

"Do you want to come to the Sweet Suite?" he says when I've learned the name of every single one.

Daredevil Toffee

"You two again," says Angie. "Hello, Mason and not-Mason's-friend."

(It's so embarrassing.)

She's turning the sign on the door to *CLOSED*.

"We've come to help," says Mason. "I won't throw a plane this time. Promise."

"Sorry, darling," Angie says. "I have to shut the shop.

I'm going to the bank."

"We can look after the shop," says Mason.

He's so happy. Probably because the first person in the world (me) has listened to the names of all his marbles.

Angie's not sure. She's wondering if it would be more trouble to get rid of us or let us stay. A family comes into the shop and Angie sighs.

"OK," she says. "Thanks very much. I'll be quick."

"Where's the toffee?" Mason says. "It's not on the counter."

"Out of sight," says Angie. "It's too chewy. I have to stop selling it. One customer lost a filling and seemed to think I should pay for a new one."

"Oh, OK," says Mason.

He's planning something. I can tell by the way his eyes are darting around. As soon as Angie's gone he digs around under the counter and takes out the jar of toffee, a pen and some paper.

"Right," he says. "We need to rebrand the toffee."

"What?"

"Rebrand," he says. "It's when you take something people don't want and describe it differently so people want it after all. It's what advertisers do. And politicians. My grandad told me."

"So if you want someone to jump out of aeroplane without a parachute," I say, "you mention the wonderful views on the way down and don't mention hitting the ground."

"Er, yes. I suppose," says Mason.

He starts his thing of speaking out loud while writing notes.

"Daredevil Toffee," he says. "So chewy it could pull the teeth right out of your mouth."

"Are you sure people are going to want that?"

"Oh yes," says Mason. "Kids will anyway. You should know that. You're a kid." He pulls a face. "Aren't you?"

I ignore him.

Mason spends ages scoring things out and starting again. The family buy little bags of liquorice and some sticks of rock and he's so busy concentrating he lets me serve them.

"Shall I mention false teeth?" he says when they've gone.

"No."

(Sometimes it's impossible to imagine how his brain works.)

When he's finished he finds some orange paper shaped like a star and writes on it (very messily) in black felt-tipped pen.

DAREDEVIL TOFFEE
EAT AT YOUR OWN RISK

So chewy it can pull your teeth right out of your gums.
PS don't worry what grown-ups think – KIDS ARE
IN CHARGE!

Then he puts the jar of toffee at the front of the counter and leans the sign against it. He looks very pleased with himself.

"Are you sure that's a good idea?" I say.

"Yes, what's wrong with it?"

I don't know where to begin.

The next people in the shop are a little boy with his dad. The boy marches up to the counter and his dad follows.

"Can I have the Daredevil Toffee, Dad?"

His dad peers at Mason's label then shakes his head. "No," he says.

"Pleeease," says the boy.

"No," he says again. "Find something else."

He looks at Mason. "Interesting approach," he says.

"Thank you very much," says Mason.

"You know," the man says to the boy, "we could go and get a hot chocolate."

The boy shakes his head. He's trying not to cry. He

wanders off to look at the other sweets.

Three little kids come in, holding change in their hands. Mason points at his sign and they run to the counter.

"I want some!" says the little girl.

She's peering up from between two older boys.

Mason smiles. "Are you sure you dare to try?" he says.

The girl nods. Mason hands her a piece of toffee and she puts it in her mouth and begins to chew. Then she chokes. The boys hit her on the back and the toffee shoots out of her mouth and on to the floor. They all run out.

Before Angie comes back there have been three crying children in the shop and one parent has asked for a refund for the Daredevil Toffee. As the dad and boy leave (without buying anything) the dad comes up to the counter.

"By the way," he says, "your sign's wrong. I'm in charge." He's not smiling.

When he's gone Mason drops the sign in the bin and puts the toffee back under the counter.

"Oh well," he says, "worth a try."

"So," says Angie when she comes back, "have you been busy?"

"No," says Mason, "pretty quiet actually."

One of life's mysteries

We're just leaving the shop when Angie says, "Oh, I think I found out about your box."

"What?" says Mason.

We run back to the counter.

"A customer told me this shop used to sell model kits," Angie says. "It was called Quarterman's. Mr Quarterman was a fisherman from Eastbourne. He and his wife retired here forty years ago. Which probably explains why the kits were in the attic."

"Where's Eastbourne?" says Mason.

"Just along the coast," says Angie. "About thirty miles away."

"Do you think the Quartermans are dead now?" he says.

"Oh I'm sure," says Angie. "They'd be very old by now."

"So how did they get the bracelet?" I say.

Angie shrugs.

"No idea," she says. "One of life's mysteries."

Fishing net

"It's not a mystery at all," says Mason as we're walking

home. "Mr Quarterman caught the bracelet in his fishing net and kept it. That's how it ended up in his attic."

"Or maybe it washed up on the beach," I say, "and he found it when he brought his boat in."

Or maybe the monster belched it up and it flew through the air and into his boat (I don't say this one).

Pink slippers

Mimi's standing on the doorstep when we get back. She's wearing a woolly coat and her pink slippers. It's getting dark.

"I want to see the, you know, the –" She's waving her arms around – "the things that arrive in the sky and change into creatures."

Mason gives me one of his looks. I pretend not to see. I don't want him making sad eyes again.

"You mean the starlings?" I say. "The murmuration."

"Yes! That! I want to see that!"

"We can go now if you like," I say, "but maybe not in slippers."

Mimi looks at her feet. "Oh," she says. "OK."

"What are you talking about?" says Mason.

"The starlings," I say. "Thousands of them come to the beach in autumn when the sun goes down. It's called the murmuration."

"It's magic," says Mimi.

And before I can stop myself I say to Mason, "Come with us if you want."

Murmuration

The sea looks like a huge grey whale slumped beneath the sky. A line of red lights dot the tops of the wind farm. A man picks up a sign for the café and carries it inside, pulling the door behind him.

The starlings come in little groups from all directions, small black arrows wheeling against the sky. They never touch. As the sun sinks down behind the horizon they merge together then spring apart, flying over the skeleton of the West Pier, twisting and turning.

Mason can't believe his eyes. He's jumping up and down. "How many are there?" he says.

"I dunno," I say. "A million?"

"Thousands anyway," says Mimi. She leans her head against my shoulder.

"It's amazing!" says Mason.

He does a little dance. (Luckily it's dark.)

More and more starlings arrive until a huge black balloon floats above the West Pier, drifting apart and then joining together again. One moment they look like a seal rolling through the sky, then they become two wriggling snakes. Then they dissolve into a fish that twists and tumbles above the old pier.

Mimi smiles. She's beautiful and tiny against the sky. I think about Mr Quarterman and his fishing boat and the two little girls who should have grown up to be friends and Mimi and her words falling away and I feel really sad and a little bit afraid.

Notes for Mimi
22. *The birds that change into creatures in the sky are called the murmuration.*
23. *Don't wear slippers to the beach. It's too cold.*

Note for me
5. *Only show interest in Mason's marbles if you have lots of time to listen to lots of information about them.*

12
UMBRELLA

Mimi's in the kitchen holding an umbrella over her head while she fries eggs.

"Morning," she says.

"Why have you got an umbrella?" I say.

"It's going to rain," says Mimi.

She looks out of the window. Grey cloud spreads to the edges of the sky. Seagulls circle overhead.

"It won't rain in the kitchen," I say.

She looks annoyed. "Do you have a problem with my umbrella?"

I don't know how to answer so I don't. I suppose it might be good to have an umbrella in case the roof leaks but it doesn't feel right.

Starlings

Mimi holding an umbrella in the kitchen stays in my head all the way to school. Mason's talking about the murmuration. He's trying to work out how many starlings there were and describing the different shapes they made. He's so busy listening to himself he doesn't notice I'm not interested. He keeps talking anyway.

As we arrive at school it begins to rain. Mimi was right about that.

Small house

It's the last school day before half-term so Miss Sharma lets us write stories. Mason spends ages gazing into space as if he might find inspiration in the corner of the ceiling. Like there might be a spider up there who will tell him what to write. My story just pours out of me. My hand can't write fast enough.

When Miss Sharma asks if I'd like to read it out I'm a bit surprised. It was really only meant for me. But I take a deep breath and begin:

"It's a small house with a small front garden with a gate that creaks, even when no one's opening it. Vines and ivy creep up the path and hang across the door so it's hard to get in. And even harder to get out."

I pause for effect and look around. Everyone's listening.

"The house is old and full of shadows. Dusty cobwebs hang across doorways, the lights are broken and the floors creak even when no one is standing on them. When it's dark outside it's dark in the little house, except if the light of the moon comes in through the window. Sometimes noises happen that can't be explained."

I'm even making myself shiver.

"Ghosts live on the mantelpiece and all the people who lived in the house before are ghosts in the shadows. And the ghosts make things appear in different places. Cornflakes turn up in the cat's bowl, umbrellas hang in the kitchen."

I stop.

"That's all I've written," I say.

"That sounds very scary," says Miss Sharma. "Where is it?"

"My grandma's house. It's where I live now."

"Well," she says, "you're certainly having an adventure."

"There's a ghost of a little girl who looks just like me. She's much younger but she's got a gap between her teeth like mine."

I look around and smile, wriggling my tongue between the gap. (Don't ask me why – I've no idea.)

Mason screws up his nose. I pretend not to see.

"You're weird," someone says from the back of the class.

Everyone laughs. Mason too.

Distracted

Miss Sharma calls me back at the end of the day.

"Is something worrying you, Iris? You seem a little distracted."

I shake my head.

"Tell me if I can help," she says. "Sharing a worry can make all the difference."

"OK," I say.

(I won't.)

"And by the way your creative writing today was excellent."

She smiles. "It was creative writing, wasn't it?"

"What do you mean?"

"No problems at home with your grandma?"

"No. It was all made up."

"Glad to hear it," she says.

Puddles

"You're quite strange, aren't you?" says Mason.

He's jumping in and out of puddles. The bottom of his trousers are soaking wet. They cling to his ankles.

"Almost as strange as your grandma," he says.

I shrug.

"Anyway," he says, "I've got something to tell you. I saw my grandad yesterday and he didn't recognise me. He asked me my name ten times at least."

"Ten?"

"Probably more like twenty. And when I was saying goodbye he asked who I'd come to visit. Like I'd just arrived when actually I'd been there for an hour and a half and I'd told him my name twenty times."

My heart gives a little scream.

"What's wrong with him?" I say.

"He's losing his memory. The doctor says it's called dementia. And I thought maybe your grandma's losing her memory too and that's why she does strange things. Even though she's probably always been a bit strange because you are. But maybe now she's going to get even stranger."

I shake my head. "Mimi's nothing like your grandad," I say. "She doesn't forget things. She just gets distracted. She's like me that way. She can remember things from ages ago. She remembers the West Pier before it burned down and she can remember meeting my grandad before my mum was even born. I wouldn't call that losing her memory."

Mason shrugs.

"And she doesn't wear shorts and a vest either," I say. "In case you're wondering."

Memories stuck to a page

Mimi's waiting for me in the hall.

"Do you want to make a little bit of magic?" she says.

And before I can answer she's skipping up the stairs.

"Come on! I've set up the darkroom."

The darkroom turns out to be the bathroom, which is full of stuff I've never seen before. There's a black blind over the window and a plank of wood across the bath with three trays of liquid on top, labelled 1, 2 and 3. A washing line hangs over the bath. The room smells of chemicals and vinegar.

The doors of the cupboard where I thought the towels

were kept is open. A big black machine with a light bulb in it is plugged into the wall.

"That's the enlarger," says Mimi. "You can't print photos without an enlarger."

She picks up a thin strip of shiny grey plastic. "And these," she says, "are negatives. You know the rolls of film you put in old-fashioned cameras? Well, when they've been processed they look like this. They're called negatives because everything is back to front. Black is white and white is black, and all the greys in between are opposite to what they actually are. We're going to turn them the right way round."

I don't understand what she's saying so I just nod.

She shuts the door, switches off the light and the room goes completely black. Then she switches on a red light.

"We have to use red light," Mimi says. "Any other light turns the photo paper black."

She's a smiling red silhouette.

She slots the negatives underneath the light bulb, takes a sheet of paper out of a box and puts it on a tray beneath the enlarger. Then she flicks a switch, the bulb goes on and light goes through the negative. Grey shapes appear on the paper. She counts to ten, then switches off the light and the room goes red again.

"Now for the magic," she says.

She lowers the paper into Tray 1 and a black-and-white picture appears. Two boys are squeezed on to a deckchair. They're both holding sticks of candyfloss. One of them is screwing up his face; the other one's smiling at the camera. They're both wearing jumpers, shorts and long socks.

"Did you take that photo?" I say.

"Yes," says Mimi. "Sixty years ago. The local paper wanted photos of bank holiday on the beach. The boys wouldn't sit still so I bought them some candyfloss."

It's sort of unbelievable. The boys gaze back at us like ghosts from the past.

"They must be old men now," I say.

She nods. "Memories stuck to a page," she says.

She lifts the paper out of Tray 1 with some tongs, drops it into Tray 2, then takes it out and lowers it into Tray 3.

"Tray 1 makes the photo appear," she says. "Tray 2 fixes the photo to the paper, and Tray 3 is water to rinse off the chemicals."

When she's rinsed the photo she pegs it to the washing line. Drops of water plop into the bath.

"Can we do another?" I say.

"Of course," says Mimi. "I think you'll like this one."

She slots in another negative, puts down a new sheet of photo paper, switches on the light, counts to ten and then drops the paper into Tray 1. Two little girls appear. The smallest one is wearing a short-sleeved dress with a white collar.

"Me and Coral," says Mimi.

I gasp. It's Coral! The girl who was eaten by the sea monster! And she's standing on the beach next to Mimi!

"Who took that photo?" I say.

"My uncle, I guess," says Mimi. "My mother didn't have a camera."

She dips the photo in the two other trays, then pegs it to the line.

Mimi and Coral are standing in bare feet on the stony beach with the West Pier behind them (before it burned down). Coral's wearing the same clothes as she is in the photo on the mantelpiece. She's crinkling her nose at the camera. It's like the photos were taken the same day. Mimi's wearing shorts and a shirt with buttons down the front and she's standing completely still. A strand of hair hangs over her eyes but she's left it there. She wants to be in focus. She's got her arm round Coral's shoulder and she's looking at her proudly.

And then I notice their hands.

"You're both wearing your bracelets!" I say.

Mimi gasps. "So we are," she says. "Isn't that wonderful?"

"So it's definitely Coral's bracelet," I say.

Mimi laughs. "Oh yes. No doubt about that."

She slots another strip of negatives in the enlarger and puts down a sheet of paper.

"You do this one," she says.

I switch on the enlarger and count to ten. Then I drop the paper into Tray 1 and a young woman in a sleeveless dress appears. She's standing next to some white cliffs looking out to sea and she's smiling to herself. She's so elegant and calm it takes me a few moments to realise who she is.

"Is that Mum?" I say.

Mimi nods.

Mum looks like another person. Partly because she's in black and white but also because she doesn't look stressed. She might even be daydreaming. Maybe she still smiles to herself when we're not there but I don't think I've ever seen her that way.

"Where did you take that?" I say.

"Don't you remember?" says Mimi. "That lovely walk we did under the cliffs. You were wearing your sleeveless dress. It was so hot we were lucky not to get burned."

She thinks I'm Mum. It's a bit embarrassing. The red light's confusing her. I don't know what to say so I dip the paper into Trays 2 and 3, then peg it to the line.

Then I say, "By the way, that's not me, Mimi. I'm Iris."

"Really?" says Mimi. "Did I call you something else?"

"Yes, but don't worry," I say.

Mimi smiles. "Do you want to do another one?"

I do. In fact, I want to do lots.

We spend ages printing photos and Mimi lets me keep them all. So I've got photos of the boys eating candyfloss in the deckchair, Coral and Mimi on the beach and Mum looking like someone completely different (I stick the one of Mum on the wall next to my bed. I like it.). I've got lots of photos of the West Pier before it fell into the sea, a photo of Grandad as a young man with his funny moustache, and a photo of me as a toddler sitting on Mimi's front step. And because I'm printed in black and white the photo of me looks like Coral.

Notes for Mimi

24. *You don't need an umbrella in the kitchen. The roof will keep the rain out.*

25. *Rena is your daughter. The girl who is staying with you is Iris. Iris is Rena's daughter.*

Note for me

6. *Tell Mason to stop going on about his grandad. There's nothing wrong with Mimi. We just printed some photos the old-fashioned way and she remembered all the chemicals and everything. And she hasn't done it for ages.*

13
November
HAND-KNITTED

I'm going to watch Mimi swimming. I'm not going in the sea myself. I'm just keeping her company. She's waiting for me by the front door and doing a little dance. She's got a blue ribbon round her finger and another tied on her basket and she's wearing red tights, a big jumper, a woolly hat and a skirt I haven't seen before. But there's something strange about her. I'm not sure what at first but then I see her skirt's inside out. White pockets flap on the front.

"Ha ha," I say. "Funny."

"What?"

"Your skirt."

"What about it?"

"It's inside out," I say.

She looks down at the pockets. "Oh," she says.

She's trying to smile but it isn't a real one. Her mouth's wobbling.

"How does it look?"

"I like it," I say. "It's different."

We're both pretending something but meaning something else.

"You always look great," I say. "You can wear anything."

And I mean it. She always looks fantastic because she's bursting with life and she's never still. Only she isn't dancing by the front door any more. She's embarrassed.

"Well," she says, "it's Inside-Out Day."

"I'll put my clothes on inside out too," I say.

"Really?"

I nod. And before I can change my mind I run up to my room.

The seagull's sitting on the shed. I want to tell her what a weird situation I'm in but I can't catch her eye. She's looking at something hanging on the washing line. She swoops down, yanks it off its peg and flies with it back to the shed. Then she bashes it against the roof and eats it. A bag falls to the ground.

I haven't got time to think about the seagull. I have to get changed before Mimi feels even more embarrassed so I turn my clothes inside out as quickly as I can. I've got ink stains on my jean pockets and my hood sits uncomfortably behind my neck. I can't believe I'm actually going out dressed like this. (It's lucky I don't have any friends.)

When I get back downstairs Mimi's turned her woolly hat and her jumper inside out. A label sticks out right above her eyes. It says it says *Hand-knitted, 100% wool.*

"You know what this is," she says as we step outside.

"What?"

"It's you giving me a vote of confidence."

I'm not exactly sure what she means but I think she's pleased.

Inside-Out Day

It's awkward at first. We bump into Lee coming home with a bag of shopping. Lola's carrying a folded up newspaper, Bonnie's got a squidgy red ball in her mouth.

"What's happening?" says Lee.

"Inside-Out Day," I say.

"Really?" he says. "What's that?"

"It's a vote of confidence."

"Well, good for you."

He takes off his flat cap, turns it inside out and plonks it back on his head.

"Is it an annual event? I'll get myself better organised next year," he says. And he waves us off.

"This is fun, isn't it?" says Mimi.

We link arms. Mimi's dancing and I'm trying to walk straight and suddenly we're laughing. It's like we're the most special, mysterious people in the world.

When we get to the beach we buy ice creams. Mimi wants one so I have one too, even though my fingers already feel like ice.

"Is there a reason your clothes are inside out?" says the ice-cream man.

"It's Inside-Out Day," says Mimi.

He hands us the ice cream. "Really? What's it for? Charity or something?"

"It's a vote of confidence," I say. "It's useful too because you don't have to wash your clothes so often."

Chocolate ice cream's dripping on to the white pockets of Mimi's dress.

"See?" I say. "All she has to do is turn it outside in and it's clean again."

We're so pleased with ourselves. We think we're so funny. Silly and happy and proud.

As we walk along the beach the deckchair lady says, "Like the outfits."

Something terrible

I'm shivering on the stones while Mimi runs down to the sea in her costume and goggles (not inside out). She kicks off her flip-flops, drops her towel and marches into the water, a thin bony figure. Then she ducks down like a seal and comes up smiling.

She swims parallel to the beach as usual towards the Palace Pier. Two small boats sit on the horizon but Mimi's the only person in the sea. I watch three joggers run along the shore and an old man throwing a frisbee for his dog. In the distance Mimi turns round and swims back in my direction. But then she stops. She's treading water. I look around to see if there's something trying to pull her under the waves but she's not panicking or calling for help. She's just bobbing in the sea, looking at the beach.

I run down to the shore, grab her flip-flops and towel and wave but she doesn't see me. She starts swimming slowly towards the beach and I race over the stones to meet her. When the water's waist-deep she wades out.

"Mimi!" I shout. "Mimi!"

She hasn't seen me. She turns and walks in the other direction. Her bare feet are stumbling on the stones.

I run after her and grab her hand. She spins round.

"Mimi, Mimi!" I say. "Are you OK?"

She stares at me, her mouth opening and shutting like a fish. I put her towel round her shoulders then I crouch down and lift one foot and then the other into her flip-flops. An awful thought's tapping at my brain and I'm having to push it away. But as we walk back along the beach it repeats itself over and over. *She doesn't know who I am. She doesn't know who I am.*

Cramp

"What happened, Mimi?" I say. "Did you get cramp?"

She's dressed now and sitting on the stones while seagulls chase each other overhead.

"I'm not sure," she says. "I…"

Her voice drifts away and she laughs. We both do. Only hers isn't a proper laugh and neither is mine. Somewhere in the laughs is something scary, something neither of us is saying. I shiver and it isn't because of the cold.

"How about some hot chocolate?" she says. "It'll warm us up."

And she takes the flask out of her basket.

Buried at sea

We stay on the beach until it's almost dark. The sun drops behind the sea, red light spilling from its edges. The starlings arrive, flocks of black darts twisting and turning against the sky. They merge into a huge toothless face that splits into drifting balloons.

Mimi's smiling now. She's feeling better.

"I think I'd like to be buried at sea," she says. "Could you arrange that for me?"

I look at her shining eyes and her hair flickering in the wind and her crinkly smile and I get a pain right across my chest.

"I want you to live forever," I whisper.

"Oh, sweetheart," she says, "have I upset you?"

She pulls me close. She's warm and bony and covered in itchy wool.

"You're my best friend," I say.

"Well, that's a bit sad, isn't it?" she says. "You can't have your grandmother as your best friend. Do something about that. That boy, for instance, he's nice."

I think of Mason scouring the beach for gold or his grandad's teeth and I feel terrible. Mason instead of Mimi would be awful.

It's like Mimi can read my mind. "Not that boy instead of me," she says. "That boy as a friend. Friends are important. And he's an enthusiast. The world needs more enthusiasts."

I don't answer. I don't say anything at all. I just want to hold on to this moment. I listen to Mimi's breathing and I breathe in time with her and slowly I calm down.

The starlings become an acrobat spinning through the darkening sky then they split apart and join together, rearing up like a lion. When they separate again they're seals jumping over invisible waves.

Glow sticks

I'm looking out of the kitchen window, thinking about what happened on the beach. Is it normal to forget things like that, to suddenly be lost? I don't know. Dad's always losing his tools. And the twins are always losing their toys and Dad's always losing at least one of the twins. But I've never known Dad to forget who I am. Never. It feel like Mimi's getting holes in her memory.

It's scary.

Flashes of light appear in the garden. Mason's crawling through the hedge covered in glow sticks. (He definitely thinks Mimi's garden is his.)

Memories

"Can I come in?" says Mason. "It's cold out here."

He's wearing gloves and a hat and at least three jumpers. And what looks like a whole packet of glow sticks.

"No," I say. "Sorry."

"I'll give you a glow stick."

I shake my head. Mimi's in her bedroom having a nap and I don't want him to come inside in case she comes down all confused. But I can't tell him that so instead I say, "Let's sit in the shed – it's more fun."

I'm forcing a smile. It's not easy. Mimi's shed is no fun at all.

"Really?" says Mason. He doesn't look convinced.

Mimi's shed is very small and full of stuff that is not at all interesting. There's a broken washing machine, boxes of plates, piles of newspaper and a wobbly stool. A torch hangs from a string. I switch it on. Mason sits on the stool and I balance on a pile of newspapers. A cobweb settles on Mason's head.

"Well, this really is fun," he says, brushing it away. "Not."

"What do you think happens if we forget things?" I say.

"Like my grandad?"

(I wish he'd stop talking about his grandad.)

"No. I just mean…"

I'm not sure what I mean. I want to talk about what happened without saying what happened.

"What are memories for?" I say.

"Well," he says, "if you don't have memories, you forget to do things. You might forget to eat your dinner or see your friends or do your homework. You just have to hope somebody feeds you."

He laughs. "My favourite foods, by the way," he says, "are sausages, pizza, ice cream, those sprinkly coloured things you put on ice cream, juice, lemonade, roast potatoes and cake."

It's like the marbles all over again. He's starting to list things.

"I'll even eat vegetables," he says. "Peas and carrots and cabbage and mushrooms, but not that horrible green stuff that looks like a miniature tree."

"Broccoli?"

He nods. "I don't like broccoli. Anyway," he says, "why do you want to know my favourite food?"

"I don't."

"You're quite funny, aren't you?" he says. "And I don't mean funny ha-ha. You ask questions and then you say you didn't ask them."

I don't argue. It was a bad idea to talk to him. I'm about to give up and go inside when he mutters something about his grandad.

"What?" I say.

"You know how my grandad didn't recognise me?" he says. "Well, he doesn't remember what he likes and doesn't like either. You could probably give him carrots, which he's always hated, and he'd eat them anyway. In fact, you could tell him they're strawberries and he might believe you."

He's blinking away little tears. "Maybe your grandma's losing her memory too," he says.

"I don't think so," I say. "She's got an amazing memory. We printed some photos, the old-fashioned way, and she remembered all the chemicals and the complicated machine and everything."

"Oh," says Mason.

"I'll show you," I say.

I run back into the house, race up to my room

and bring down the photo of Mimi and Coral on the beach.

Mason shines the torch on the photo and stares and stares. "Coral's wearing the same clothes," he says. "It's like the photo on the mantelpiece."

"Yes," I say. "It might be the same day. And look at their hands. They're wearing the bracelets."

"Wow! That's amazing," he says. "How did you make the photo?"

I try to explain but I can't.

Fish

We don't stay in the shed for long. It's too cold. As Mason's about to crawl back through the hedge he pulls a bag out of his pocket and puts it in my hand.

"Just a thought," he says, "but if your grandma's going to hang fish on the washing line, you should train the seagull to put its rubbish in the bin."

Ants

It takes me ages to get to sleep. My head's full of worries. They're crawling out of the corners of my brain like ants, creeping into everything. Why is Mimi wearing her clothes inside out and not noticing? Why did she not recognise me on the beach? Why did she hang the fish on the washing line?

I keep pretending everything's OK when actually I feel as though there's a little hole in my heart and it's getting bigger. And I'm not sure everything's OK at all.

Notes for Mimi

26. *If you can see the inside of your pockets or the labels on your clothes when you're wearing them, they are probably inside out. Which is OK if it's Inside-Out Day.*

27. *The girl who goes to the beach with you is called Iris. She's your granddaughter.*

28. *If you hang fish on the washing line, the seagull will eat it and drop the litter.*

14
COLD BRIGHT SKY

Mason wants to go back to the museum shop to see if they've got more marbles. I'm going too. I want to see the girl in the film. Mimi's made me a packed lunch.

"Malcolm," she says when Mason arrives, "I've made enough sandwiches for two if you're hungry."

"Thanks," says Mason, "but my mum made me some."

We walk out under the cold, bright sky.

"Let's go to the beach and get some chips," says Mason, "in case the sandwiches are rubbish."

Long shadows

We sit on the stones near the little hut where they smoke fish. It's cold but the sun's so bright, bouncing off the sea, that we have to look sideways. Long shadows stretch out behind us. We're sharing a bag of chips. Seagulls fly in circles above us.

"The funny thing about the sea," says Mason, "is you always have to look at it. Like you never see a line of deckchairs facing away from the sea. Even though it's really interesting with the little shops and stuff."

"Mimi says we're made of water," I say. "That's probably why we can't stop looking at it."

"Why do you call her Mimi?" says Mason.

"Dunno," I say. "We all do."

"Does your whole family talk to the moon?" he says.

(Every time I think he's OK he reminds me how annoying he is.)

"Maybe," I say.

We finish our chips and Mason shakes the scraps out of the bag. Four screaming seagulls swoop down and squabble over them. They cry sixty-seven times without a gap.

"Right," says Mason. "Marbles."

He jumps up, puts the bag in the bin and runs ahead. "Come on!" he shouts.

And suddenly I'm running too, past the people taking selfies, the toddlers wrapped in enormous coats, the buggies, the dog walkers and teenagers on skateboards. A little boy's blowing bubbles and they float through the air. Mason jumps up and pops one. I do the same. And as we run we pick up bits of rubbish and stuff them into the bins.

We run up to the main road, catching the green light perfectly, and race up through the shops and the market. Eventually, when we can't run any more, we walk. The sky's blue, and a seagull calls thirty-eight times and I feel really happy.

Doppelgänger

The museum shop has got marbles in for Christmas. Mason's so excited you'd think he's found his grandad's teeth. While he's choosing (which will take ages) I go up to the small cinema to see the film of the girl who looks like me. The loop's at the bit where the boy in the blue jumper is sliding down the helter-skelter. Then comes the girl in the yellow cardigan and the green dress. She goes really fast, stops at the bottom, smiles at me and waves. I wave back (I can't stop myself). Then she freezes. Then she's gone.

She still looks like me. My face, my teeth, my smile, my red hair. And I still don't know what to think. I go to find someone to ask. The woman I spoke to last time is standing by the stairs.

"Yes, lovely?" she says.

"You know the film?" I say. "Can you come and look? One of the children from long ago looks like me. It's a bit confusing."

"Let me see," she says.

We sit together and watch the film.

When the girl appears I say, "Her. What do you think?"

"Well, she does look rather like you," says the woman. "She could be your Doppelgänger."

"What's that?"

"Your double. Some people think we all have doubles. And every now and then we bump into one or someone thinks we're someone else. It happens here," she says, "in the museum. Occasionally someone comes in and I recognise them from another visit but it turns out they haven't been before."

"Really?" I say. "That's spooky."

She smiles. "Thing is," she says, "if that girl turned in

the other direction you might see she has a much bigger nose than you or a smaller chin. So she might not look like you at all if she's facing another way."

She stands up. "I'm sorry I can't be more help," she says. "Interesting, though."

As soon as she's gone Mason swoops into her seat. He's holding a bag of marbles.

"Look!" he says. "I got some really good ones!"

He looks at the screen and yawns. It's coming round to the helter-skelter again. "Not this again. Boring."

And then he screams. Actually screams right in my ear.

"She's wearing the bracelet!"

I stare at the girl, but before I can be sure she's gone.

"That girl's wearing the bracelet!" he says.

His eyes are like gobstoppers.

"Is she? Is she?"

"I'm not kidding," he says. "The whistle's sticking out of her sleeve. Wait and see."

We watch the film again and there's the girl sliding down the helter-skelter, stopping at the bottom, smiling her gappy-toothed smile and lifting her hand to wave. And poking out from under her sleeve is a green whistle and what looks like red beads. I can hardly believe my eyes.

"Is that really Coral's bracelet?" I say.

"Looks like it to me," says Mason.

"But why's she wearing it?"

Mason shakes his head. "Dunno."

And then we have the very same thought and we both shout it out at exactly the same moment.

"That's Coral!"

Cheese

We watch the film over and over, peering at the girl's wrist, until we're absolutely sure she's wearing Coral's bracelet. Mason's so excited he's forgotten to show me his marbles. Eventually we go down to the picnic room to eat our lunch.

"Are you sure that's not your grandma in the film?" says Mason.

"No," I say. "Mimi had brown hair. Me and Mum got the red hair. And Coral."

"Well, it must be your mum," he says.

"It can't be my mum. The film says 1954. My mum wasn't even born then."

Mason shrugs. "Well your grandma's got her dates wrong," he says. "Because Coral's about ten in that film. Not two. So the boat must have sunk much later."

I feel really sorry for Mimi and a bit embarrassed.
I don't want to talk any more so I get Mason to show
me his marbles. Unfortunately he's got quite a lot.
When I've looked at every single one we eat our lunch.
Mason has crisps, juice, yoghurt, and cheese and
tomato sandwiches. I have juice, an apple, a spoon
and stale sandwiches cut into triangles – with
nothing inside. No butter. No cheese. Just stale bread.
Mason thinks it's hilarious.

Fish

Mimi's emptying everything out of the fridge and putting
it back again. She can't find the fish and she wants it for
tea. I don't tell her about the girl in the film. I think she'll
be embarrassed. And I don't tell her she hung the bag of
fish on the washing line either.

Instead I say, "I don't want fish anyway. Can we have
something else?"

She thinks for a moment. "We could have sandwiches,"
she says, "for a change."

Sweet girl

The sandwiches are stale like the ones I had for lunch

but at least they've got cheese in them. Mimi's cut them into triangles and laid them in a circle on a plate so they look like a flower.

"Isn't this lovely?" she says. "Delightful company and delicious sandwiches."

Most people wouldn't really describe the sandwiches as delicious. In fact, if it was a café, you would write on the menu *NOT delicious sandwiches served in a tiny dining area by an old lady who will join you at the table.*

"You do know this is a fancy restaurant, don't you?" she says. "And we've got the window seat looking out to sea."

"Of course," I say.

"And there's no chance of the seagulls wanting to steal our chips because we're not eating chips," she says. "We're eating an afternoon tea on tiers of plates."

She gazes at the plate as if there's a feast laid out in front of us.

"There are cakes and biscuits on one layer, scones on another layer," she goes on, "and sandwiches on another. And the seagulls can't swoop down and help themselves because we're behind a window. Now, would you like a seaweed sandwich or a shell sandwich or perhaps a sandwich filled with the finest stardust?"

"Cheese sandwich please," I said helpfully.

She holds out the plate and I help myself. The seagull calls from the roof twelve times.

"Do the seagulls get any?" I say.

"Oh yes," she says. "There's a girl working here who's a bit clumsy. She's always dropping things but she's a sweet girl and anything she drops she keeps for the seagulls. They wait behind the restaurant and when she goes out to the bins they pad over to her. She's taught them not to make too much noise in case the chef comes out and tells her off so they're the quietest seagulls in Brighton."

"What's her name?" I say.

"Rena," says Mimi.

"That's Mum's name."

"Well, she's the sweet girl. When she was a teenager she worked as a waitress and she was always dropping things. She lost her job after a couple of weeks. She didn't mind, though. She got another job looking after the deckchairs. And it doesn't really matter if you drop a deckchair. As long as there's no one underneath it."

It's a strange thing to think of Mum as a sweet girl. There was obviously a whole other Mum before I came along.

"Anyway," Mimi says, "what kind of tea would you like? Stardust tea or elephant-poo tea or seagull-feathers tea?"

I don't want tea today. Not with rubbish sandwiches.

"Can I have some juice?" I say. "Or water?"

"Good choice," she says, and ignores me.

She picks up the teapot, holds it over my cup and pours out a stream of orange juice.

We both laugh but I honestly don't know if she meant to do it or if she's as surprised as I am to find juice in the teapot. It doesn't matter, though. She's still the nicest, silliest person I ever met.

We sit for ages imagining places we might like the restaurant to be. Mimi thinks it would be nice to be in a desert or up a mountain. I imagine being in a snow-covered forest or by the side of a lake, but in the end we always come back to the sea – the white waves crashing on to the shore and the tier of plates getting emptier and emptier.

Notes for Mimi

29. *The boy next door is called Mason not Malcolm.*
30. *If you don't put anything in between slices of bread, they are not really sandwiches. They're just slices of bread.*

31. *Iris likes orange juice in the teapot. Do it any time you want.*

Note for me
7. *Don't tell Mimi about the film. She'll be embarrassed.*

15
CROCODILE

Mimi won't go swimming. She hasn't been since she didn't recognise me on the beach. I want her to go so everything feels normal again.

"Are you going swimming today?" I say. "I'll come."

"No," she says. "I'm going for a walk with Lee. Anyway, I thought you didn't like swimming."

"I like watching," I say. "I just don't like going in myself. I'm not a good swimmer."

Mimi rolls her eyes. "How did I manage to have a granddaughter who doesn't like swimming?" she says.

"Maybe the twins will do better. I'd like to think so."

A lump fills my throat. It's holding back a sob. I don't care if the twins do better. Really I don't. But something's making me want to cry.

"I'm not like you," I say at last. "I think you're part fish."

"Really?"

"Or a mermaid," I say. "You're probably a mermaid. I'm more like a camel. I don't belong in water."

Mimi smiles. "You're fine," she says. "You're just a bit of a crocodile. You don't like to go in too deep."

She stretches out her arms and snaps her hands together and then she's chasing me out of the kitchen, laughing. I'm laughing too. We run into the living room and collapse on to the sofa. Thomas squeals and shoots out of the room. It's really funny.

But we laugh a bit too loud and a bit too long and as we do something changes and we're not exactly laughing any more. I can only describe it one way. It's like we're pretending everything's fine while all around us huge waves are trying to pull us under.

Raindrops

When Mimi goes out with Lee I take some boxes from

my room and empty them on to the floor. Then I check every single photo. I want to find a picture of ten-year-old Coral so I can show Mimi. I won't give it to her exactly, I'll just prop it up on the mantelpiece so she sees it. That way she'll remember Coral without me having to tell her.

Outside the sky darkens and raindrops trickle down the window. I imagine Mimi, Lee and the dogs caught in the rain. Lola with her long dripping hair and Bonnie sheltering underneath and getting wetter and wetter. I go through three boxes of photos as quickly as I can, then put them back. Mimi will be home soon. I've found nothing.

Doorstep

Lee's standing on the doorstep. Water's running off his hat and dripping down his nose. Lola and Bonnie are wet and shivering.

"Has Mimi come home?" he says.

"No."

"We lost each other on the beach," he says. "Bonnie ran off and by the time I found her Mimi had gone." He flashes a smile.

"She's not here," I say.

"Oh, well, not to worry," he says. "I'll keep looking."

He turns and walks down the path, the dogs trailing behind him, and a little knot forms in my stomach.

Cats don't like cake

The house feels extra empty not knowing where Mimi is. I imagine a storm rolling in from the sea and Mimi walking close to the shore. I hope the lifeguards are out because she's so thin she could easily be blown over and carried off on a wave. And then she'd be gone.

When the doorbell rings I run to the door. Mum and the twins pile in, wet and soggy.

"Where's Mimi?" says Mum.

"She's out."

"And left you on your own?"

"I am ten," I say, "not four."

"Glad to hear it," she says.

She gives me a kiss. The twins grab my legs and try to pull me over.

I follow Mum into the kitchen, trying not to let the twins trip me up. It's like wading through a storm. She fills the kettle and rinses the teapot. Pearl points at Thomas's bowl and screams. There's chocolate cake in it.

"Thomas has got cake!" she yells.

"Oh, I did that," I say. "I thought it would be a treat."

"Really?" says Mum. "Surely you know chocolate makes cats sick."

(I do know that.)

She tips the bowl into the bin.

"Are you sure you're not four?" she says.

"You're silly," says Noah. "Cats don't like cake!"

"Silly, silly," repeats Pearl.

If you're happy and you know it

The longer Mum and the twins stay, the harder it is to imagine Mimi ever coming back. We sing "If You're Happy and You Know It" with all the actions (the twins especially love stamping their feet). Then we play musical chairs with me doing the music and the twins fighting over who gets to sit in the one chair. It ends up with them both crying. Eventually I get tins of food from the kitchen cupboard and put them on the living-room floor. The twins roll them across the carpet and build towers with them and for a while they're happy. I take the bracelets from the mantelpiece and sink on to the sofa next to Mum.

"Look," I say. "We found Coral's bracelet."

"Mimi's cousin?" says Mum.

I nod.

She takes them from me and turns them in her hands.

"How amazing!" she says. "I had no idea Coral had a bracelet."

"It's got *CB* carved on it for Coral Butterworth," I say, and I point at the bead. "We found it at the flea market."

"Wow!" says Mum. "How extraordinary." She's shaking her head.

"What do you know about Coral?" I say.

"Nothing really," says Mum. "All I know is she died on a boat trip with her parents."

"How old was she?"

"I don't know," says Mum. "She really wasn't discussed when I was growing up. Too sad I suppose. The first time I saw a photo of her was when Mimi put that one on the mantelpiece."

Pearl comes over, slides on to Mum's lap and reaches for the bracelets.

"No, Pearl," says Mum, "they're not for you."

"I want them!" says Pearl.

She tries to pull one out of Mum's hands and I imagine the string snapping and the beads flying across the room.

"You can't have them," I yell. "Stop being so spoilt!"

I prise Pearl's fingers apart and take the bracelet. She

howls. Mum mutters, "For goodness' sake," and Noah's tower of tins crashes to the ground.

I put the bracelets back on the mantelpiece, go into the kitchen, take a deep breath and wait. The rain looks like it will never stop.

Very nice man

The third time the doorbell rings it's Mimi. I'm so relieved. She's standing on the doorstep completely soaked. Her hair's sticking to her face and water's dripping off her coat.

"I just met a very nice man," she says, "with two dogs. He was wearing a flat hat."

"That was Lee," I say. "He was looking for you."

Mimi frowns.

Mum appears in the hall.

"At last," she says. "I thought you were looking forward to seeing us."

She sounds like she's about four years old herself. All hurt feelings.

"I did tell you I had the afternoon off."

Mimi's staring at her. She looks confused. Noah and Pearl run up. Pearl trips over at Mimi's feet and begins to cry. Mum picks her up and carries her back into the living room.

Mimi presses her mouth to my ear. "Who are these people?" she whispers.

A shiver runs down my spine. It's as if she's been abducted by aliens.

Tins

Mum's washing some mugs at the kitchen sink. Mimi's sitting at the table while I dry her hair with a towel. The twins are back in the living room playing with the tins. Everything's calm.

"So," says Mum, "how was your walk?"

"Fine thank you," says Mimi. "How was yours?"

"We didn't walk," says Mum. "We jumped on the bus. Just as well given the weather."

Mimi looks up at me and mouths, "Who is she?"

I mouth back, "Rena."

"Who is she?" she repeats, this time louder.

"Rena," I say.

"Yes, sweetheart?" says Mum, turning round. "Not like you to call me Rena."

It's an awful moment. Mimi closes her eyes. I smile and keep rubbing her hair with the towel. Mum looks puzzled. She pours tea for her and Mimi and we sit round the table in silence. Mimi won't talk and I don't want to make things worse so I don't talk either. Mum's looking annoyed.

When the twins come running in it's a relief. They hold out their hands and little bits of torn coloured paper fall through their fingers.

"Look what we've done," Pearl says proudly.

"We did it," says Noah. "We did it!"

They run back into the living room and we follow. The tins lie on the floor, their labels scattered across the carpet.

"They fell off!" snorts Pearl.

Noah picks up a handful of paper and sprinkles it on the floor as if he's feeding the birds.

"How will I know what's in each tin?" says Mimi.

"You won't," says Noah. "It's a surpriiiiise."

Pearl's so excited she picks up a tin and throws it into the air. It comes down on her head. There's a tiny (almost invisible) bit of blood and lots of screaming.

"OK," says Mum, "time to go home."

Her voice sounds like a bit of elastic being stretched and stretched. She wrestles the twins into their coats and bundles them out of the door and into the rain. Thunder roars in the distance.

Thunder

Mimi's staring at the tins and torn paper.

"I'm really sorry," I say. "I shouldn't have let the twins play with them."

"I never know what's inside anything anyway," she sighs.

"No one does if the labels are gone."

"But I don't seem to have labels for anything," she says.

I shudder. I've got a terrible feeling. I don't know what she means and I don't want to know either. I try to hug her but she pushes me away. Lightning flashes in through the window and Mimi spins round, picks up the china cat I bought her and throws it across the room. It hits the wall, smashes into pieces and rolls across the carpet. Thomas jumps up and runs out of the room. Thunder crashes. Mimi stands for a moment, her mouth open, then she slumps on to the sofa.

She sits for ages, saying nothing, while the sound of thunder fades into the distance. She's staring at the china cat's head. It's lying by her feet.

Then she says, "Did I do that?"

I nod.

"Oh well," she says, "I don't like cats anyway."

Thomas pokes his head round the door then creeps back into his basket. Mimi looks at him blankly. She doesn't remember I bought the china cat for her. She'd never have thrown it if she remembered. I'm trying not to mind but I do.

On the roof the seagull calls – *kee-yah kee-yah kee-yah kee-yah kee-yah kee-yah kee-yah kee-yah kee-yah kee-yah*. Twelve times. I wonder if she's telling me the cat broke into twelve pieces. Anyway, I can only find eleven.

Notes for Mimi

32. If you go out with Lee, you should come back with him.

33. The people who came round are your daughter, Rena, and her twins, Noah and Pearl. Noah and Pearl are Iris's brother and sister. Rena is Iris's mother.

34. The nice man with the flat cap and the dogs is Lee who lives over the road. He's your friend.

35. You do like cats. You've got a black-and-white cat (not very friendly) called Thomas.

36. You also like cat ornaments and the one you threw was the one Iris gave you.

Notes for me

8. Don't buy ornaments for Mimi – she can't remember

getting them, probably because she's got so many.

9. *Don't let the twins play with Mimi's tins ever again!*

16
THIS MAN IS MY HUSBAND

I don't go into Mimi's bedroom to be nosy. Really I don't. I just want to check she's all right. Because after she threw the ornament she looked so sad. And then she went upstairs to lie down.

I knock on her door but she doesn't answer so I pop my head round. And she is all right. She's asleep on her bed, snoring. And if the rest of her house looks like a shipwreck, her bedroom does too. There are books all over the floor and falling off shelves and covered in dust and there are clothes on top of the books and there's a dressing table covered in ornaments and hand cream and ribbons.

And stuck to the walls and lying on every surface are little notes written in Mimi's spidery writing. I pick one up off the carpet. It says *Don't put peas in cake.* I put it on her bedside table and read some of the others. Here's what they say.

The girl in the next-door bedroom is Iris. She is your granddaughter. She is ten years old. Iris doesn't like swimming.

Iris's mother is Rena. She is your daughter. She is married to Jim.

Iris doesn't have a job. She goes to school.

Rena and Jim also have twins called Pearl and Noah. They are two years old.

The men over the road are Lee and Danny. They walk the dogs. They are your friends.

The boy who crawls through the hedge is called Malcolm.

Cake tins are in the drawer with the yellow ribbon.

Yellow ribbon on apron and oven gloves.

Eggs go in cakes.

If you can see the label, your clothes are inside out (wrong way round).

Don't wear slippers to the beach.

No need for an umbrella in the kitchen.
Starlings on the beach are called the murmuration.
Cats eat cat food. There is a picture of a cat on the tin.
Put sugar into cocoa. Not salt.
Tins (baked beans etc.) and dried food go in the cupboards.
Cold food goes in the fridge.
Frozen food (frozen peas, ice cream etc.) goes in the freezer compartment at the top of the fridge.
Keep the fridge door shut or the cat might take the fish.
If you leave the fridge door open, it will whistle.
Swimming – blue ribbons.
Take basket, swimming costume, thermos flask, goggles, towel – two if Iris is coming.

And she's written down days of the week with instructions, so Monday is *recycling collection* and Wednesday is *rubbish collection* and weekdays say *Iris goes to school*. But the days are muddled up, so Tuesday comes after Friday and Thursday and Saturday have fallen off the wall. She's put names on the photos on her dressing table too, so on Grandad she's written *This man is my husband*.

And every note I read makes me feel more worried so by the time I see *This man is my husband* I feel like something really heavy is sitting on my shoulders. I creep out, close the door and go to my room and sit on my bed so the heavy feeling will go away. But it doesn't. It gets heavier.

The seagull on the roof calls twelve times. I don't know what she's trying to tell me, but if she thinks Mimi's only written twelve notes she's wrong. There are probably twelve x twelve notes (144). At least.

Wet and horrible

I think Mimi's memory isn't working. It's like little bits of it are disappearing so things don't make sense any more. She didn't recognise Mum or the twins or even Lee. And she can't remember Coral at all, even though Coral lived to be at least ten years old. And she can't remember to put eggs in cakes or sugar in cocoa.

I have to talk to Mason. The more I think about Mimi, the worse I feel and there's no one else I can tell. I run downstairs and crawl through the hedge into his garden. It's cold and wet and horrible. I'm surprised he does it so often.

Mason's sitting at the table in his house looking bored. When he sees me he jumps up and opens the kitchen door.

"Come in!" he says, like I'm the most exciting person he's ever met.

Different shades of white

Mason's house is painted all different shades of white. Some walls look like white in sunlight and some look like white in shadow, some look like snow when it's turned to sludge and some look like white needing a bit of a clean. And there are no pictures or ribbons or shelves covered in stuff. It's like a dentist's room without the reclining chair and all the drills.

"It's quite boring, isn't it?" Mason says.

"Is that why you like coming to Mimi's?"

He nods. "Anyway," he says, "what do you want?"

I take a deep breath. "I think Mimi's losing her memory. She's got notes on her bedroom wall about everything she mustn't forget. She's even got my name written down in case she forgets it. She's got me down as *the girl in the next-door bedroom*."

"Sounds like my grandad," he says.

"No," I say. "Not like your grandad."

"Well, at least your grandma's got her teeth," he says. "They haven't been dropped into the sea by a seagull. They don't have fish laying eggs in them."

I try to smile but I can't. I'm beginning to wish I hadn't come round.

"She's got you written down too," I say. "She calls you *the boy who crawls through the hedge* and she says your name's Malcolm."

Mason snorts. "I like the name Malcolm actually. It's unusual. She can call me Malcolm if she wants. You can too, if you like. Or you can call me Colm, if you prefer."

I glare at him. I don't know why he has to try to make everything funny.

Mason raises his eyebrows. "If everything I say is wrong, why do you even want to talk to me?" He's looking annoyed.

"I'm sorry," I say. "I want to help Mimi but I don't know what to do."

"Have you told her about Coral being ten?" says Mason.

"No."

"Tell her," he says. "It might bring her memories back."

"Do you think so?"

"Well," says Mason, "you can't expect to be a good athlete if you don't train. Maybe it's the same with memory. Maybe you have to practise. If I knew something

191

my grandad had forgotten I'd definitely tell him."

I'm not very sure it's a good idea but I can't think of anything better.

"OK," I say. "I'll do it tomorrow."

"I'll come round and help," says Mason.

Dancing

Mimi's dancing in the kitchen like nothing went wrong yesterday at all. Like she didn't forget who everyone was and she didn't throw the china cat. Thomas is draped over her shoulder and she's waiting for the kettle to boil. You might think Thomas wouldn't like this (especially after Mimi was so rude about cats) but he doesn't seem to mind. When Mason knocks on the window Thomas gives him a look as if to say *Mimi loves me best.* Then he jumps down and walks out of the kitchen.

"Malcolm," says Mimi, "how lovely to see you. Would you like some breakfast?"

"Yes please, Iris's grandma," he says.

(Yes he says that.)

Mimi laughs. "Do call me Mimi," she says.

"OK," says Mason.

I'm sure he won't. Because if he did, he'd have to start calling his grandad Albert or Cornelius or whatever his name is.

We sit round the table and eat toast and jam. Mimi tells us about Lee teaching her yoga and Mason talks about his mum's driving lessons (she's got her test soon). I'm trying to think of a way to mention the girl in the film without sounding awkward.

Mason keeps looking at me. Then he says, "We had an interesting visit to the museum when I got my marbles, didn't we, Iris?"

"Yes," I say. "In fact –" I look at Mimi and the words pop out (awkwardly) – "I think you've got the date wrong for when Coral died."

"Really?" says Mimi.

"We saw her in a film at the museum and she's about our age," I say.

Mimi shudders. "And how old are you?" she says.

"I'm nearly eleven."

"I'm nearly eleven too," says Mason.

"The girl in the film's wearing the bracelet," I say, "and she looks like me. She's even got red hair. And that's why we think she's Coral. And the film says 1954, so she can't be Mum. Because Mum wasn't even born then."

Mimi shudders. She looks like her thoughts are wading through mud. Her face crumples.

"Everyone gets things muddled," says Mason. "I'm always getting my socks muddled. I get dressed and I think everything's fine but when I take my shoes off I find I'm wearing one blue sock and one green. Or a stripy sock and a sock with no pattern, or a new sock and an old one with a hole so my toe's poking out."

He's about to start reciting one of his lists. I give him a look. He doesn't notice.

"And sometimes," he says, "I put on one of my mum's socks and one of mine. And that's terrible. Because then I've really muddled things up and they could end up in the wrong drawers. And one time when my grandad used to visit—"

I kick him under the table. Hard. I don't want him talking about his grandad. I want him to stop talking this very moment.

"Right," says Mimi.

Her face looks like it's being blown by slow-motion winds. It's moving all over the place. She gets up and walks out of the kitchen.

"Oh dear," mutters Mason.

A cloud wraps itself round us. I wish I hadn't said anything. Seeing Coral in the film doesn't feel exciting or interesting any more. It feels awful.

Secondary school

Me and Mason sit for ages but we don't say another word. Mason tries to look at me with sad eyes but I ignore him.

Eventually he gets up to go. As he does he whispers, "By the way, don't tell your mum and dad your grandma's forgetting things or they might not let you stay."

It's a horrible thought.

"And then we wouldn't be friends any more," he says, "because we're only friends because we live next door and you'll find a proper friend when you go to secondary school." His mouth's wobbling.

"Actually," I say, "I think we are friends. If that's OK."

"Really?" says Mason.

I nod.

"OK," he says. "That's OK."

And he's gone. Out into the garden and through the hedge.

Note for me

10. *Don't tell Mum and Dad about Mimi forgetting things. Especially don't tell Mum – she'll want to move back into her old bedroom.*

17
FRIGHTENED

It's our first day back at school after half term. Mimi's sitting at the kitchen table in her dressing gown and slippers. She's gazing out of the window.

"Do you want a cup of tea?" I say.

She shakes her head. "No thank you."

I sit down beside her. "Toast?"

She shakes her head again.

The seagull's sitting on the shed, staring at the washing line in case someone might hang another bag of fish there. She calls twelve times. She's probably saying twelve bags of fish would be better than one. (She's going to be disappointed.)

Mimi turns to me. "Iris," she says, "I'm frightened."

My stomach lurches. Mimi being frightened is terrifying. I feel about two inches tall, like Thomas could easily bat me under the table, sit on me and then carry me into the garden.

I take a few deep breaths. "What are you frightened of?" I say.

"I'm frightened because I can't remember a thing about Coral. You said you saw her aged ten but I've got no memories of her at all." She screws up her face. "Which is terrible," she says. "How can I forget someone who was so important to me?"

"We could go to the museum and I could show you the film," I say. "Then you might remember."

Mimi shudders. "No. What if I didn't remember? It would be too upsetting."

She tries to smile but she can't. "Thank you, though," she says.

Parent helper

I feel bad. I don't want to leave Mimi. Mason doesn't notice though. He's jumping along the pavement, bursting with excitement. Our class is going litter picking and his mum's coming as a parent helper. Most kids would be worried about that but not Mason. He can't wait.

"She's fun," he says. "Everyone will like her."

"Well, you're lucky then, aren't you?" I say. "Because my mum's no fun at all. And we've got twins. And they spoil everything."

"I wish we had twins," says Mason.

I ignore him. He's got no idea what they're like.

As we cross the road Lee comes out of his house with the dogs.

"Morning," he says.

"Morning," I say.

And then, before I can stop myself, I say, "By the way, Mimi was fine after you lost her on the beach. In case you were wondering."

"Oh, good," says Lee.

"I think she was enjoying the walk," I say.

"Lovely," says Lee.

"In fact," I say (I wish I'd shut up), "she only got lost because her glasses were covered in spray. From the sea and the rain. But as soon as she took off her glasses she knew exactly where she was."

(Yes, I say that. The words just pop out.)

Mason snorts. Lee smiles. We're all staring at each other, waiting for something. The moment seems to last forever.

At last Mason says, "We have to run now, if you don't mind."

He starts jogging on the spot. "I'm timing myself to the end of the street," he says.

"Go on then," says Lee. "I'll count."

Mason starts running not very fast along the pavement. When he reaches the end of the road Lee calls out, "Twelve seconds! Well done. Not bad at all."

"Do you want to do the same?" he says to me.

The honest answer is not really but I've told him so many lies already I might as well tell another.

"Yes please," I say.

And I run to the end of the road. Also not very fast.

"Fifteen seconds," Lee shouts.

I turn and wave and we walk round the corner and out of sight.

"Why are you so weird?" says Mason.

Embarrassing

Mason's mum looks like Angie but not like Angie. It's

like they started off with the same face but they got pulled in different directions so Angie's face is more square and her nose is longer. And Mason's mum doesn't have the nose ring.

And the strange thing is she goes to the front of the line and stands next to me and Mason. And Mason doesn't mind at all. In fact, he's happy. Which is not at all normal, because kids usually hate having their parents at school because they're bound to do something embarrassing. Mason isn't embarrassed, though. He keeps taking her hand.

And Mason's mum does something embarrassing almost immediately. As soon as we walk out of the playground she tries to match her footsteps with Mason's so when he has his left foot forward she has her left foot forward and when he's got his right foot forward so has she. But because Mason keeps stopping to look behind us (we're at the front because he's Eco Rep) his mum keeps having to do a funny little dance to get her feet in the right place. It's awkward.

But after a while I'm doing it too. I can't help it. It feels weird not to. And by the time we get to the seafront the whole class is trying to match their steps with Mason's, even Miss Sharma. And no one's sneering. In fact, everyone's laughing. I can't really understand what's happened.

Litter picking with the school is completely different from me and Mason litter picking on our own. We're all wearing yellow jackets and gloves and we're each given a litter picker, which is a stick with a handle. When you squeeze the handle, little claws at the end of the stick pick up whatever's underneath. So long as it's not too heavy. You can't really pick up stones with it (everyone tries) and we're not meant to grab each other (everyone tries that too) but they're great for little bits of plastic.

The class spreads across the beach and after an hour we've filled three huge bags with plastic bottles, wrappers, coffee cups, tins, sweet packets and loads of little bits of stuff that have broken off something else. We don't find Mason's grandad's teeth or gold or, in fact, anything exciting at all, just loads of rubbish that would stick in the seagulls' throats and poison the fish.

"Excellent job," says Miss Sharma.

As we walk back to school Mason's mum does her matching steps thing again and everyone does it behind us. And when we're back in the playground she shouts "Bye" to everyone and does a funny little wave. And everyone waves back.

"Told you," says Mason.

Feathers

I worry about Mimi all afternoon. I keep thinking about all the things she might be doing and all the things that might be going wrong. I feel like her house is made of feathers and even the slightest breeze (or sneeze) will blow it away and by the time I get home from school it will be gone.

"What's the matter?" says Mason as we walk out of the gates.

"I'm worried about Mimi."

"Why?"

"In case she left the cooker on or the tap."

"What about if she left the window open, or the front door?" he says. "She might have done that. Or fed the cat to the seagull."

"It's not funny," I say.

He shrugs. "It is a bit."

We run home. Well, I do, and then Mason follows and overtakes me, and then I overtake him, and then we race. By the time we get to Mimi's we're laughing and everything feels a little bit better.

Magic powers

"Malcolm, would you like to stay for tea?" says Mimi.

She's smiling. Happy.

"Yes please," says Mason.

Mimi opens the kitchen cupboard. It's full of tins with no labels. All silver. All identical. For a moment I think she's going to get upset. But then she laughs.

"We'll have a lucky dip," she says.

She takes some tins, puts them on the table and Mason chooses one.

"I think this is custard," he says.

He gives the tin to Mimi who closes her eyes and weaves her hands over it as if she's casting a spell.

"It's not custard," she says at last. "It's peaches!"

When it's my turn I shake the tin. I'm trying to work out if there's something large slopping around in there or something small. It feels like something small.

"Baked beans," I say.

Mimi opens the tin. Sticky syrup drips down the sides. Peach slices float on top.

"Ha ha!" she says.

Mason chooses another tin, shuts his eyes like Mimi and says, "I'm getting a feeling it's tomato soup."

Mimi does her spell-weaving thing again.

"Vegetable soup," she says. "It's vegetable soup."

I pass the tin from one hand to the other. It feels like something small in liquid again.

"Chickpeas," I say.

(I'm hoping not.)

It's vegetable soup. Mason's gazing at Mimi as though she's got magic powers.

"How did you do that?" he says.

"No idea," says Mimi.

I think the last tin's grapefruit. Mason thinks it's pineapple chunks. Mimi thinks it's toothpaste. (She's losing her magic powers.)

It's tinned tomatoes.

For tea we have bread and butter with tinned tomatoes heated up with vegetable soup, followed by cold tinned peaches. And it's really nice.

Time machine

I finish my persuasive writing before I go to bed. Miss Sharma told me to try to write something positive so I'm not going to list all the reasons my life would be better without the twins. (It would take too long anyway.) Instead I write about a time machine.

Why Scientists Should Invent a Time Machine

All scientists should work together to invent a time machine. Lots of people would be helped by this for lots of different reasons. These are my reasons.

I would like a time machine so I can go back in time and visit my grandma Mimi and her cousin Coral when they were very small. I would like to do this so I could stop Coral and her parents getting on the boat that sank. That way Mimi would still have a cousin and Mimi and Coral would have been friends for life.

My second reason is that if I could go back in time I would give Mimi a diary and tell her to write down all her memories so she would never forget them.

And my third reason is that I would like to play on the beach with Mimi and Coral just for one day. I would be very happy if I could do that. And if Mimi wrote about our day in her diary I could read about it later too.

I know it's possible that if we change the past other things we don't like might happen instead, but if I had a time machine that wouldn't matter. I would keep going back until things were perfect.

Please can this be arranged? A time machine would be a wonderful scientific creation and it would make lots of people very happy.

Note for Mimi

37. Toothpaste comes in tubes not tins.

18
ORANGE WELLINGTON BOOTS

Dad's coming round with the twins and I've invited Mason. If he thinks they're such fun, he can try spending a few hours with them. He helps me tidy before Dad gets here in case Mimi's done anything odd. Mimi thinks he's the nicest boy in the world.

The surfaces are all scrubbed, there's cat food in Thomas's bowl and cake in the cake tin, and Mimi's clothes are the right way round.

But when Dad arrives he's carrying Noah who's got a bloody bandage on his head and is flopped over Dad's shoulder. He's wearing a Spiderman costume and one sock.

"Oh dear," says Mimi. "What happened?"

"He was climbing the banisters," says Dad, "and he fell. I need to get him checked. I'm meeting Rena at the hospital. Is it OK if I leave Pearl with you?"

"Of course," says Mimi.

Pearl's wearing bright orange wellington boots. When she sees Thomas in the kitchen doorway she gets down on the floor and pretends to be a cat. She's crawling down the hall meowing.

"So cute," says Mason.

"Take off your boots and coat, Pearl," says Dad.

"No," says Pearl.

Mason gets down on the floor and starts meowing too and eventually, after lots of meowing and lots of fuss, he pulls off her boots and coat.

"Thanks," says Dad. He looks exhausted.

"Pearl's brought her jigsaw, haven't you, sweetheart?" he says.

And then he's off out of the door carrying Noah.

Jigsaw

Pearl tips her jigsaw on to the living-room carpet. It's a

picture of a farmyard with animal-shaped holes and lots of little animal shapes that fit right in. Like the sheep fit in the sheep shape and the cow in the cow shape and the three little chickens in the little chickens shape.

"That's a lovely jigsaw," says Mason.

"Cow," says Pearl and she picks up a black-and-white cow and pops it into the cow-shaped hole.

"Cat," says Mimi, and points at the goat.

"That's not a cat!" says Pearl.

"It is," says Mimi. She's gritting her teeth, quite annoyed.

"It's not," says Pearl. "It's a goat."

Mimi looks worried.

"Cats don't have horns," says Pearl. "Do they, Iris? They don't have horns."

"No, it's a goat," I say.

"OK," says Mimi, "if you say so."

Pearl picks up the goat and slots it into place.

"Shall we play something different?" says Mason.

"No," says Mimi. "I think I can manage a two-year-old's jigsaw."

"My turn," says Pearl (again). "Rabbit."

Mimi shakes her head.

They're about to fight over a rabbit. I can't stand it any longer. I'm going to pretend I'm Mum and hide in the kitchen and make a pot of tea.

As I wait for the kettle to boil I hear them all laughing. I walk back down the hall and peer round the living-room door. Mason's showing off his dance moves and Mimi and Pearl are copying (sort of). They've got no idea how embarrassing they look. Like if anyone else could see Mason he'd be teased for the rest of his life. I smirk but they don't notice. And then I feel a bit jealous. And I don't even know why. I can't help it.

Mason sees me and stops. "Do you want to play hide-and-seek?" he says.

"OK," I say.

"Me and Iris can count," says Mason, "and you two can hide."

It's the worst game of hide-and-seek ever. Mimi's feet stick out of the bottom of the curtains. Pearl sits in the corner with a cushion over her face.

"You need better hiding places," I say. "We'll count to 200 so you can find somewhere good."

Me and Mason wait in the kitchen.

"Sorry about Pearl," I say. "You can see how annoying she is."

"She's fun," Mason says. "I don't know why you complain."

He hasn't been here long enough to see the worst

of her. And anyway, if both twins were here he'd feel completely different. I don't say that, though. I just shrug.

We count slowly up to 200. Then we shout, "We're coming!"

Cobwebs

We can't find Mimi and Pearl anywhere. We look under the chairs and behind the coats and curtains and in the wardrobes and cupboards. I even open the fridge. We check the kitchen and the living room and I search my room and Mimi's room (it's too embarrassing to let Mason in there) but they're not there.

Mason crawls through the hedge to check they didn't go into his garden but they're not there and he checks his house but they're not in there either. No one is. And they're not in Mimi's shed. Not hiding under piles of newspapers with their feet sticking out or sitting on the stool with cobwebs in their hair.

We stand in Mimi's hall and call their names. I'm trying not to panic.

"Pearl!"

"Mimi!"

"Pearl!"

"Mimi!"

"I'm making hot chocolate!" I shout. "Do you want some?"

(That would normally get Pearl to come out but there's no answer.)

And then I notice Pearl's orange boots and coat are gone. And I have a horrible, horrible feeling. I open the front door and look down the street. It's getting dark. The wind carries a paper bag down the gutter.

"I think they've gone out," I say.

We walk on to the pavement and look in both directions but they're not there.

"My grandad went missing once," says Mason. "The police found him sitting on a park bench miles from home."

I glare at him.

"Just saying," he says. "He was all right. He was happy sitting there. The police said he was singing. It was everyone else who wasn't happy."

"What's that got to do with Mimi?" I say.

"Because," he says, "maybe you should call the police. Or the lifeguard."

I shake my head. I don't want to call the police because then everyone will know Mimi gets muddled. And there'll be a huge fuss. "No," I say.

"Check Lee and Danny's then," says Mason. "She might be there."

We run across the road and bang on their door but there's no answer. Not even Lola or Bonnie barking. There's no one in.

"We have to find her ourselves," I say.

My heart's doing its screamy thing.

"OK," says Mason, "where would she go?"

"The sea," I say. "It's her favourite place. She wants to be buried there."

Mason makes an *uh?* sort of face. Any other time he'd snort.

"Come on then," he says, "we'd better run."

White lights

We run as fast as we can, our feet slamming against the pavement, and as we do I realise we didn't even shut the front door. But I don't go back. Because nothing matters any more. Not having no friends, not the damp on my bedroom wall or the annoying twins or my distracted, stressful mum. Because in one split second the whole world's gone from OK to terrifying. And nothing matters except finding Mimi and Pearl.

We run down the lanes, past clothes rails being wheeled

into shops and shopkeepers pulling down shutters. When we reach the seafront the wind is so strong it's hard to walk into it. A sheet of plastic tied across some scaffold flaps and tugs at its ropes. We wait for the lights to change, then drag ourselves across the road, pushing into the wind, down the slope and on to the beach.

The beach is almost empty. White waves crash on to the stones. The sun's a red ball sinking behind the horizon. Flocks of starlings drift across the sky. Seagulls screech. The strings of white lights along the promenade twist and swing.

The lights on the Palace Pier flicker in the distance and a girl wheels her bike along the cycle path, leaning against it so the wind doesn't blow it over.

Mason's trying to say something.

"What?" I shout.

"You check the shore!" he yells. "I'll search the top of the beach!"

And before I can answer he's running off, his hair tangled in the wind, a silhouette racing around the empty restaurants, in and out of sight.

For a moment I'm frozen, but then I'm running down to the water's edge, my feet twisting on the stones. Waves crash on to the beach, churning up spray and rattling the stones. Something huge and dark moves through the sea and my stomach lurches. The sea monster's got them! I'm sure!

I take a deep breath and scream. "Mimi! Mimi! Mimi! Mimi! Pearl! Pearl! Pearl!"

The roar of the sea swallows my words.

And then I see a flash of orange along the beach. Mason's seen it too. He's waving. He runs down to the shore and I follow him and we race together over the stones. As we get closer the orange becomes a small pair of wellington boots. Two silhouettes stand together, blown by the wind.

"Mimi!" I scream. "Pearl!"

Pearl's holding on to Mimi's skirt. Her face is flat and frozen like the wind has blown all expression out of it. Mimi's face is too old to be all blown out but it's collapsed like a balloon with the air drifting from it.

I crouch down in front of Pearl and hold out my hands. "Pearl," I say, "shall I carry you?"

She nods. I pick her up and she wraps her arms round my neck. Her nose is cold and wet against my skin and I don't mind one bit. I'm trying not to cry.

"Come on, Mimi," says Mason. "The moon's waiting for you at home."

It's the first time he's ever called her Mimi.

Mimi points up at the sky. The moon's appearing

from behind a cloud.

"It's here," she says. "Look."

"Yes," says Mason, "but it's too windy here. It's nicer in your garden."

He puts his arm through hers and leads her up the beach. I glance at the sea and squeeze Pearl tight. Then I follow.

"The monster won't get you now," I say.

"What monster?" says Pearl.

"The sea monster," I say.

"You're silly!" she says. "There's no sea monster."

She's laughing. And I laugh too. And then suddenly I'm crying.

"Silly," she says. "You're silly." She's blowing bubbles into my ear.

Above the West Pier three flocks of starlings merge into a boat rocking on stormy seas, then circle in on themselves like a cat chasing its own tail.

19
FROWN

Dad's standing in the street. His hair's weaving around in the wind and his face is doing the same. I'm still carrying Pearl. Mason's holding Mimi's hand.

"The door was open," he says. "Everything all right?"

I nod.

A frown wriggles across his forehead. Pearl reaches out and pulls herself into his arms.

"Is Noah OK?" I say.

"Yes," Dad says. "They sewed him up. He's fine. I've dropped him home with Mum."

Mason turns to Mimi. "I've got to go now," he says, "but the moon's waiting for you."

Mimi nods. Her hair's hanging in front of her eyes. Mason pushes it back off her face. Then he points up at the sky. A silver sliver of moon hangs between the clouds.

"There it is," he says. "Look."

Over and over

Mimi goes straight into the garden to talk to the moon. The seagull calls from the top of the shed.

Kee-yah kee-yah kee-yah kee-yah kee-yah kee-yah kee-yah kee-yah kee-yah kee-yah kee-yah kee-yah.

Kee-yah kee-yah kee-yah kee-yah kee-yah kee-yah kee-yah kee-yah kee-yah kee-yah kee-yah kee-yah.

Over and over.

One day at a time

Me and Dad are squeezed together on the sofa, Pearl's asleep beside us. Thomas is curled up in his basket. Mimi's gone to bed.

"So," says Dad, "are you going to tell me what happened?"

"We were playing hide-and-seek," I say, "and Mimi took Pearl down to the beach. I'm not sure why and I think maybe she got a bit lost."

The words sound shocking.

"She's done a few odd things lately, hasn't she?" Dad says. "Been a bit forgetful."

I nod. "Please don't tell Mum," I say. "She'll want to lock her up or something."

Dad frowns. "You're very hard on your mum, aren't you? She only wants the best."

"Yes, but she's always imagining the worst."

"Bit like you then," says Dad.

I pout. I feel two years old. I want to be two years old. I lean my head on Dad's shoulder. I miss him.

"Of course I'll tell Mum," he says. "Mimi's her mother and you're her daughter."

Tears fill my eyes. I wipe them away but everything's blurred.

"What if she does more strange things?" I say.

"Then we take one day at a time," says Dad. He sighs. "Sometimes it's best to live in the moment. I know you're always waiting for some perfect time, Iris, but this might be the perfect time."

I sink my face into his jumper and breathe in the smell of bananas and soap. We sit for ages.

Then he says, "Can you show me the bracelets before I head home?"

I take the bracelets from the mantelpiece and give them to him, then I run up to my room and bring down the photo of Coral and Mimi.

"I printed this with Mimi," I say.

"In the bathroom?" says Dad.

I nod. "Did you know she did that?"

Dad smiles. "Mimi used to do a lot of printing at home," he says. "Rena often helped."

"Look, they're both wearing their bracelets," I say, pointing at Mimi and Coral.

"That's wonderful," says Dad.

Pearl gives a little snort and shudders awake. She looks like she's about to scream.

"Hey ho," says Dad. "Home time."

Not my family

Mum's taking Mimi to see a doctor. She's having everything checked. She's had her eye test (needs stronger glasses), her aches and pains are normal (she's old). Today it's something else. She drives me and Mason to school on the way, dropping us off at the gate. As we walk into the playground Mimi gets out of the car and waves.

"Have a good day, sweethearts!" she shouts. "Live, love, learn."

It's extremely embarrassing.

"Not my family," mutters Mason as we walk through the playground.

It makes me glad I usually walk.

Invisible

I give Miss Sharma my time machine writing. She likes it. I don't want to read it out to the class so she pins it to the wall.

"Iris has done a wonderful piece of writing about wanting scientists to invent a time machine," she says. "What she's actually talking about is hindsight – knowing what's going to happen before it actually does. Can anyone think of something else we could use to help us predict the future?"

"History," someone says.

"Yes!" says Miss Sharma. "One way to think about what may happen in the future is to look at what's happened in the past."

Mason puts up his hand. "Having a superpower," he says.

"Um, yes," says Miss Sharma.

"I do actually have a superpower," he continues.

(I think he should stop talking now. He doesn't.)

"I can make myself invisible," he says, "if I shut my eyes, I disappear."

"We disappear, idiot," someone says. "If you shut your eyes, you can't see us. We can still see you."

Everyone laughs.

Mason shuts his eyes. "See, you've all disappeared," he mutters.

His face is hot but he's not giving up.

The laughing gets louder.

"All right, all right," says Miss Sharma. "That's enough. Good answer, Mason. I think you mean you can make everyone else disappear. Well done."

No one else thinks it was well done and Mason knows it. When the bell goes he races out of the classroom.

I run out after him. "I thought that was sort of clever," I say, "that thing about making yourself invisible."

"No you didn't," he says.

Marzipan carrots

I arrive home from school just as Mum's coming out of Lee and Danny's house. She looks upset, like she's a puppet and all her strings have come loose. Her mouth's upside down and her eyebrows are drooping.

"Iris," she says, and she puts her arm round my shoulder.

Inside, Mimi's asleep on the sofa. I kiss the top of her head, then follow Mum into the kitchen. A cake from a supermarket sits on the table. It's decorated with marzipan carrots.

"Cake?" says Mum.

"No thanks."

"OK," she says.

She fills the kettle and waves it around absent-mindedly. Drops of water splash on to her shoes.

"What's wrong?" I say.

She hesitates for a moment.

Then she says, "Mimi's losing her memory."

My heart starts doing somersaults.

"What do you mean?"

"The doctor told us her memory isn't as good as it was. It's called dementia."

I suppose I already knew but I feel like I've been catapulted around the room and I'm bouncing off the walls. I nod really slowly, trying to stop the moment.

"Would you like to come home with me?" Mum says. "Rather than stay here?"

"No! Why would I want to do that?"

I have to stop myself shouting. I don't want Mimi to hear.

"I've been here two months," I say, "and it's fine."

"It's not that fine," says Mum. "Mimi could have lost Pearl."

"She didn't lose Pearl," I say. "And anyway, Pearl's two. I'm nearly eleven. Mimi's perfect for me. In fact, we're the same age really. Inside."

My eyes fill with tears. It's like being under water, though my feet are still touching the ground (just about).

Mum's crying too. I can see that much.

"I remember things for her," I say. "And we have fun together."

Mum sighs. "I think I was always too old for Mimi," she says. "Even when I was a child. You're probably perfect."

"I am perfect," I say. "Didn't you know?"

I'm trying to smile.

Mum puts the kettle down, walks over and we hug. It's the sort of hug I want to last forever.

"You won't make any secret plans, will you?" I say. "About Mimi's future? Or mine."

"No," says Mum. "I promise. So long as you say if you have a problem. Lee and Danny are going to keep an eye on Mimi. And you. But you must ask for help if you need it. Or if you're worried about anything. Can you promise?"

"I promise," I say.

"OK," says Mum.

Then she puts on her coat, kisses Mimi goodbye and heads for the door.

Tea and cake

"Why so sad?" says Mimi.

We're sitting on the sofa. I can't look at her. I might cry.

"What?" she says. "What's wrong?"

"Mum says you're not very well," I mutter.

"I am well!" she says.

She jumps to her feet. "Look at me!"

She's does a little dance in the space between Thomas's basket and the sofa. Her feet are sliding around in her slippers. The photo of Coral flutters down to the carpet. She picks it up and puts it back on the mantelpiece. Then she sits down again.

"I didn't need a doctor to tell me my memory's playing up," she says. "I've known for a long time."

"Oh," I say.

"How could I not know?" she says. "Lee and Danny know too, I'm sure. And probably the dogs. I once ordered them tea and cake."

"The dogs?"

She laughs. "Yes. In a café. It was a little awkward."

I don't know whether to laugh or cry.

"Sometimes," she says, "it's like a fog comes down and I'm not sure what's going on. But mostly I'm fine. And now's fine. I can do a little dance and you can keep being adorable. Can we live with that?"

I think of Lee saying *Where else would I be?* And I nod.

Beard and baggy trousers

Mimi goes across the road to see Lee and Danny and I write down the word because I don't want to say it out loud. I'm going to let Mason read it. I know he'll say something stupid and then it won't feel sad any more. So I write *DEMENTIA* on a bit of paper, fold it up and put it in my pocket. Then I crawl though the hedge.

Mason's in his kitchen doing some dance moves. Normally I'd let him see me laughing (sneering), but instead I pretend not to notice. I tap on the window. He breakdances to the door.

"Do you want some carrot cake?" I say.

He's nodding furiously.

He charges through the hedge behind me and we sit at the kitchen table and gaze at the perfect, beautiful cake.

"Mimi didn't make it, did she?" Mason says.

I shake my head. I don't say it, but I'm thinking, *No, because this one doesn't look like a massive burnt biscuit.*

Instead I say, "Mimi's like your grandad."

"What do you mean? A beard and baggy trousers?"

I hand him the folded paper. Half of him is interested, but the other half just wants cake. His eyes keep sliding towards it.

"Read it," I say, and he does.

"She's got dementia?"

I nod.

"That's sad," he says.

I wonder if he's kidding. I'm waiting for him to laugh or run his finger round the icing but he doesn't.

"Do you want some cake now?" I say.

"Yes please."

I cut him a huge slice and put it on a plate.

He eats it all without saying a word. I'm not sure he's enjoying it.

Notes and ribbons

Mason eats so much cake he feels sick. Then he goes home. When Mimi comes back she kisses me goodnight and goes straight up to bed. I put on my pyjamas, brush my teeth and crawl in beside her. She's already asleep.

The night seems to last forever. I lie there surrounded by notes and ribbons with Mimi snoring next to me, and every time I shut my eyes they spring open again.

Because nothing feels right. It's like someone's taken a story and thrown all the pages into the air so they're completely muddled up. Mimi's memories are disappearing. The little girl who looks like me lived to be ten years old but Mimi can't remember a thing about her. And it took a two-year-old to tell me there's no such thing as a sea monster.

When I finally fall asleep I dream of starlings and seagulls and lost girls jumping over marzipan carrots. Until eventually it's morning.

20
ANCHORS

I write my notes for Mimi on two sheets of paper and take them downstairs. She's in the kitchen washing up.

"Mimi, I made these for you," I say.

She turns round. "For me?" she says.

I nod.

She dries her hands on her apron, takes the lists, sits at the table and begins to read. I'm afraid to look in case she's annoyed.

"Did I really hang the fish on the washing line?" she says.

"Yes," I say, "the seagull ate it."

"Well, I hope she enjoyed it," she says.

When she's finished reading (it takes a while), Mimi stands up and holds out her hands.

"Fancy you doing that for me," she says.

"You're not cross?"

"Of course not. When you're drifting out to sea you need as many anchors as possible. And these will be my anchors."

She puts her arms round me and we hold each other tight and I imagine waves crashing around us while we keep ourselves afloat. Then she goes into the living room and comes back with a roll of tape and another sheet of paper. She tapes my lists to the fridge and the third sheet next to it.

"You know that paper's blank?" I say.

Mimi rolls her eyes. "Thank you, Iris. I do know. But it won't be blank for long."

Don't wear your apron to the beach

The paper stays blank for about ten minutes. Then Mimi goes for a walk with Lee. She steps outside in woolly tights, boots, a skirt, a jumper and her apron. I take the apron, give her her coat and put a hat on her head.

Then I start the new sheet.

Note for Mimi

38. An apron won't keep you warm in November, especially on the beach. Take a coat.

Boxes

Mason's helping me search Mimi's photos. We've got to find one of Coral aged ten (or at least not two). It just might bring Mimi's memories back. When Mason sees how many boxes of photos there are in my room his mouth falls open.

"Well," he says, "I hope they're interesting."

We search one box at a time, spreading the photos out on the floor. And Mason finds them all really interesting. At first anyway. He looks at every single photo. He doesn't just pick them up and glance at them then put them down – he has a proper look and says something about them. And then he puts his favourites in a pile. It takes ages.

Mason's favourites are:

Children jumping on a bouncy castle next to the beach.

People queuing up to go in the bingo hall on the Palace Pier.

A man balancing deckchairs on his shoulder.

The murmuration spread out over the skeleton of the West Pier.

People sitting in deckchairs on the Palace Pier eating ice creams.

A seagull sitting on a red lifebuoy on the beach.

The wind lifting up a deckchair and throwing it into the air.

Mimi aged about ten, wearing a waitress's frilly hat and apron that are too big for her. On the back of the photo someone's written *Mimi Butterworth*.

But the only photo of Coral is from when she was two years old standing on the beach in her dress with the white collar.

"Oh well," says Mason. "At least we tried."

He's had enough. He wants to go home.

Lemons

Mimi's standing in the hall in her coat and hat, holding a pair of gloves. She's looking worried.

"I think these are Lee's," she says.

"I'll take them," I say and I grab them and run out of the door.

I catch Lee as he's walking up his path. Bonnie's

standing by the gate, her ears twitching; Lola's pushing a ball along with her nose.

"Iris," says Lee, "how are you?"

"I'm sorry I didn't tell you the truth about Mimi," I say. "She did get lost on the beach that time."

(The words fall out in a rush.)

"I know," says Lee. "Don't worry. Though next time please tell us if things go wrong."

I nod.

"Do you think if I find some memories that Mimi's lost she might get better?" I say.

"I'm not sure it works like that," says Lee, "though old memories are always good to have. Especially happy ones. I'm sure Mimi would love some more happy memories."

"OK," I say.

I give him the gloves and he takes his keys out of his pocket. He's about to go inside when my last (and most terrifying) question pops out.

"What do you think will happen?"

He smiles.

"There's an expression," he says. "*If life gives you lemons, make lemonade.* Have you heard of that?"

"No."

"It means make the best of what life throws at you.

233

You might think lemons are a bit sour, you might prefer strawberries, but if you've only got lemons make lemonade."

"Oh," I say.

(I think I know what he means.)

"And that's what will happen," he says. "We'll make lemonade. Me and Danny and you and your family. We'll do our best."

He opens his door and they all go inside, Lee in his little pool of still air, Bonnie's ears twitching and Lola pushing the ball over the step and into the house.

While I can still remember

There's an envelope on my bed. It's got my name written on it in Mimi's spidery letters. I open it.

Dear Iris,
While I can still remember I thought I'd tell you a few things about me.

I used to be ten. Really I did. I had the longest hair. I wasn't allowed to cut it. And one day I found a pair of scissors and lopped it all off. My mother was furious. It was just me and her at home so I couldn't get away with anything. If there'd been twelve children, she might not have noticed one of them had cut her hair.

When I was eleven I wanted to be an astronaut. Even though no one had gone to the moon yet. Except for a dog.

I was twelve too once. That'll be you soon. I loved being twelve. I used to help my mother clear the tables in the West Pier restaurant and afterwards she and I would walk along the beach. And sometimes we'd swim.

Your grandad, the man I married, was very sentimental. He cried when you were born and when you said your first words and took your first steps and any time you did something funny or clever or silly. When you were small you always made sure he had a glass of water by his side. In case he got dehydrated. And when we watched the West Pier fall into the sea we both cried.

Your mum, Rena, was a lovely child. I called her Rena because the letters also spell near (I don't think she knows that) and I wanted to keep her near to me. And she's always stayed near, my Rena.

I enclose a photo of a younger me. Your grandad took it. I had just come back from taking photographs on the beach. I was careful to stay very still because I wanted to be in focus. I think it's a good one.

With all my love,
Mimi x

I shake the envelope and a black-and-white photo falls on to the bed. It's Mimi as a young woman, standing by her front door, holding a camera. She's wearing a very short dress printed with flowers and knee length white boots. And she's completely still apart from her feet, which look like they're tapping.

Rooftops

Mimi's sitting on the sofa in the living room. It's getting dark outside.

"Thanks for the letter and the photo," I say.

"You're welcome," she says. "Thanks for being you."

I sit down next to her and together we watch as darkness slides into the room. The moon sits in the corner of the window.

"Did you always talk to the moon?" I say.

Mimi smiles. "Oh yes. All my life. Don't you?"

I shake my head.

"Of course you don't," she says. "You talk to the seagull. But the nice thing about the moon is there's only one and it's not going anywhere."

A flock of starlings soars through the sky, settles on the houses across the road and then flies up over the rooftops towards the sea.

Dreaming

I'm reading in bed when I hear tapping on my window. It's bound to be Mason. I jump up and pull back the curtains. He's standing on the flat roof wearing his pyjamas and a woolly hat and waving a sheet of paper. He looks like he's about to explode. I open the window and cold wind blasts into my room.

"Coral didn't drown on that boat!" he hisses. "Mr Quarterman rescued her!"

"What?"

"The man who had the model shop! He rescued her. I did a search for Coral Butterworth and I found this. I printed it for you!"

He shoves the sheet of paper into my hands and then he's gone, padding across the flat roof and pulling his window down.

Sea Urchin

Mason's printed out a newspaper article. It's dated August 1946. This is what it says:

On the afternoon of 8 May 1946 a strong gale was blowing with an unexpectedly heavy swell after a calm sunny morning. Off the coast at Rottingdean the pleasure boat the *Sea Urchin* was in difficulties and struggling to stay afloat. A fishing vessel from Eastbourne, the *Blue Moon*, saw the stricken boat and hurried to her side, arriving just as the *Sea Urchin* capsized. Despite great difficulties, the *Blue Moon* managed to rescue all but two passengers. The youngest child rescued was a two-year-old girl named as Coral Butterworth. Unfortunately the child's parents were lost. Brave hero Harold Quarterman is highly commended for his actions.

I have to read it three times before it makes sense. But then it does. Sort of. Mimi was right! The boat did sink when Coral was two! Only Coral was rescued by Mr Quarterman! And that must be how he got the bracelet. But what happened next?

I switch off my light and look out of the window. The seagull's sitting on the top of the shed. She looks at me, her eyes glinting.

"Coral didn't drown on that boat," I whisper. "She lived to at least be ten. She might even have moved in with Mimi and her mum. Only Mimi's forgotten."

The seagull nods then cries twelve times. She might be saying, *Doesn't surprise me in the least,* or she might be telling me Coral lived to be twelve years old.

Sleep

When I finally fall asleep Coral slips into my dreams. Sometimes she's two years old standing on the beach holding an ice cream and sometimes she's playing with Mimi and sometimes she's sliding down the helter-skelter on the West Pier in a green dress and a yellow cardigan. Smiling, smiling.

And sometimes she's me.

A proper mystery

Me and Mason talk about the newspaper article all the way to school.

"At least we know how Mr Quarterman got the bracelet," says Mason. "Coral gave it to him."

"Yes," I say, "except Mr Quarterman rescued her when she was two and the girl in the film is our age. And she's still wearing the bracelet."

"Maybe Coral was in two sinking boats and Mr Quarterman rescued her twice," says Mason.

"I doubt it," I say. "That would be a bit unlucky for Coral, wouldn't it? Anyway, Mr Quarterman was a fisherman. Not a coastguard."

"Do you think Coral moved in with Mimi?" says

Mason. "And Mimi's forgotten."

"I suppose so," I say. "There wasn't any other family."

"Ask your mum," Mason says. "Maybe she knows."

"I did ask her. She said no one ever talked about Coral. All she knows is that she died when a boat sank."

"You don't think your mum's forgotten too?" says Mason.

I think of Mum with her antennae always twitching, never missing anything, and I shake my head.

"My mum never forgets anything," I say. "If someone told her about Coral, she'd never forget."

We stare at each other for a few moments.

Then I say, "Whatever happened, we've got find out so we can tell Mimi."

Twenty-pound reward

We're looking after the Sweet Suite while Angie sorts out her Christmas decorations upstairs. A woman comes in. She's got curly hair poking out of a woolly hat and she looks worried.

"I'm sorry to bother you," she says. "I lost my keys this morning. Could I put a notice in your window?"

"I'll ask," says Mason.

He runs to the back of the shop and up the stairs.

"Would you like to buy some sweets?" I say.

(I'm thinking they might cheer her up.)

"No thank you."

"I can give you some toffee for free."

She shakes her head. "No thanks. Really."

I'm glad actually. It would probably ruin her day and it's already a bit spoilt.

When Mason comes down he's holding a roll of tape. "My aunt says I can stick it in the window for you."

"Thank you," says the woman.

She hands Mason a piece of paper. It says:

HAVE YOU FOUND A SET OF KEYS?
£20 REWARD.

Underneath there's a phone number.

"Twenty pounds!" says Mason when she's gone. "We should look for the keys ourselves."

I'm nodding but I'm not thinking about the twenty pounds. I'm having a brainwave.

"Why don't we make a poster asking for information about Coral?" I say. "We can stick a photo on and put it in the window. If Angie doesn't mind."

Mason gasps. "Great idea!" he says, and he's running up the stairs again to see Angie.

When he comes down he's beaming. "She said yes!"

"I'll ask Mimi if we can print a photo in the darkroom," I say, "and you can come too."

Proper dark

Mimi's worried she'll forget how to set up the darkroom but she remembers everything exactly right. Mason squeezes in with us so the bathroom feels really small. It's definitely not designed for three people. Especially if one of them is Mason. When Mimi puts out the light he screams.

"Wow! I've never been in this much dark before. This is real, proper dark."

He's jumping around all over the place. It's a relief when Mimi turns on the red light.

We print the photo of Coral standing on the beach holding her ice cream, only we print it bigger than the one on the mantelpiece. As she appears on the paper, squinting at the sun, we can see the bracelet on her wrist and a little drop of ice cream trickling down her hand. Mason can't believe his eyes.

"Wow! Wow! Wow!" he says.

Do you remember this girl?

We don't tell Mimi we're going to make a poster but when she goes out with Lee we stick the photo of Coral on to a sheet of paper. Then we write:

Do you remember this girl?
Her name was Coral.
If you have any information, please come into the shop.
There is a reward.

The reward is Mason's idea. He wants it to be toffee but if an old person comes in with information we're going to make it Parma violets. In case they don't have any teeth.

Angie lets us stick it on the shop door.

"I'll hang some tinsel round it," she says.

21
December
NOTHING HAPPENS

Nothing happens. No one goes into the Sweet Suite to say they remember Coral. The shops fill up with Christmas things and me and Mason help Angie fill shiny Christmas stockings with sweets and sticks of rock.

Dad finishes filling the holes in the bricks to stop the mould and the scaffold comes down from the back of the house. Now he just has to paint my room. And Mimi starts putting her own notes on tins and cupboard doors and clothes and clocks.

Christmas lights go up in Brighton, stretching

through town and along the seafront, and Mum and Dad check on Mimi as often as they can. (Too often. Mum definitely wants to move in.) Mason's mum passes her driving test and takes Mason up the observation tower on the beach to celebrate. He thinks he sees a shark. (I think he doesn't.) I make my model planes and me and Mason fly them over the hedge to each other until they fall apart. Lee or Danny come round most days and Lee and Mimi go for lots of walks with the dogs. And sometimes Mimi loses her parachute and sometimes she doesn't, and I never know which it's going to be but I don't mind either.

And mostly she's fine.

Flap their wings

At school Mason reads out his persuasive writing. He stands up and takes a little bow. Then he begins.

"Dear head teacher," he says. "Daredevil Toffee from the Sweet Suite is the best, chewiest toffee in the world. I recommend that this school gives every child Daredevil Toffee at least once a term."

He's looking very serious.

"My first reason for this," he goes on, "is that these lucky children would be sure to work hard in lessons because they would be so happy about the toffee. Although some people think children eat too many sweets, I believe that a little treat once each term would do much more good than harm. It would also make this school the most popular school in Brighton.

"My second reason for giving Daredevil Toffee to children is it is so sticky it would lock their teeth together so classes would be quiet for at least half an hour each term. Teachers could also be given Daredevil Toffee as a reward for all their hard work. This would make the classrooms even happier as they wouldn't be able to tell the children off.

"And, finally, eating Daredevil Toffee is a rare experience that everyone should try at least once in their lifetime. It really is one of the wonders of the world."

He pretends to chew. He looks really funny. Everyone's laughing.

"And what makes it extra special is it's made by the seaside and blown dry on the beach by seagulls who fly above it and flap their wings."

He flaps his arms.

"And guess what?" he goes on.

He takes another little bow.

"It still tastes like toffee."

Everyone laughs. Even me. He's proud.

"That was good," I say as we walk home.

Star biscuits

Mimi's out with Lee and Danny and I'm making star-shaped biscuits when Mason appears at the kitchen window. He's jumping up and down, waving his arms about. He looks like he's falling off a trampoline. When I open the door he crashes into the kitchen waving a note.

"Coral's been into the Sweet Suite!" he shouts. "She's alive!"

"What?"

He holds the bit of paper in front of my eyes. "Read that!"

The note says *Coral Quarterman*. There's a phone number underneath.

"I don't understand," I say. "What does that mean?"

"It's Coral," says Mason. "Mimi's cousin. She went into Angie's shop and left her number. She's alive!"

"But she's been dead for years," I say. "She can't suddenly be alive."

"She is alive! She's an old woman now. Angie met her."

"But it says Coral Quarterman?"

Mason shrugs. "Maybe Mr Quarterman adopted her," he says.

And suddenly everything falls into place. Mimi doesn't remember Coral because Coral wasn't there. Coral was with the Quartermans.

I start dancing around the kitchen. I don't even care that Mason can see me.

"Mimi will be so happy," I say.

"Call Coral!" says Mason.

But I can't. I'm too scared.

"Go on. Call Coral!"

"I can't," I say. "I really can't."

I'm not even sure why. It just feels too scary.

"OK," he says. "Get your mum to do it then. And tell me what happens."

"I will!" I say. "I will!"

"And give me some biscuits," he says.

I give him all the biscuits he can carry. Which is a lot.

Something's happened

I'm not going to tell Mimi about Coral yet because I'm worried the message might be a joke or a mistake or something might go wrong. I wander around the house for ages trying to calm down. And then I text Mum: *Please come over after work. Something's happened.* Then I send another text saying, *A good thing,* in case she thinks something terrible has happened and she has to move in with me and Mimi.

She calls me straight back.

"Are you OK, Iris? Is Mimi OK?"

She sounds like she's caught in a storm.

"Yes," I say, "something happened but it's good news. Just come. And don't tell Mimi I called you."

Exhausting way

Mum comes as soon as she can, rushing over in that mad exhausting way of hers so I can almost feel her arrive before she gets here. When I open the door she falls into the house with the twins.

"Sorry," she says. "Dad's painting your room. I couldn't leave them."

The twins grab my legs and try to pull me over. It's like being dragged down by three foot waves.

Mimi appears in the hall. "What a lovely surprise," she says. "Do you two want to watch *Chitty Chitty Bang Bang*?"

"Yes, yes! Yes!"

They let go of me and run into the living room and clamber on to the sofa.

"Don't play the same bit over and over, Mimi," I say.

"Why would I do that?" she says.

Surprised

When I tell Mum we've found Coral she can't think who I'm talking about. We're sitting at the kitchen table. Mum's got her chin resting on her hands. She's looking confused.

"Mimi's cousin! The girl in the photo," I say. "She didn't drown."

"The girl with the bracelet?" says Mum.

I nod.

"Sorry, sweetheart, I don't understand."

I don't really want to explain. I just want Mum to call Coral but I need her to know what happened. So I tell her the whole story right from the beginning. I tell her about the red-haired girl in the film at the museum who's about ten years old and looks like me and I tell her about Mason buying Coral's bracelet at the flea market. And I tell her that the cardboard box the bracelet came in was from Quarterman's model shop. And I tell her that Mason's aunt has a sweet shop at that address now and she found the box in her attic. And I tell her about the photo of Mimi and Coral as little girls on the beach both wearing bracelets and how we went back to the museum and saw the girl in the film wearing the bracelet. And that's how we knew Coral lived to be ten years old. And I tell her about the newspaper article saying Mr Quarterman rescued Coral. And finally I tell her about the poster we put up asking for information with Parma violets as a reward (I probably didn't need to tell her that bit).

And then I say, "And a woman went into the shop and left this note and she said she was Coral! So that means Coral didn't die after all."

Mum frowns and for a moment I think she's spotted an obvious mistake and it's going to be so embarrassing when she points it out. But she doesn't point anything out.

Instead she says, "Wow, Iris. Aren't you amazing?"

"It wasn't just me," I say. "It was Mason too. He lives next door. And he's in my class. He found the bracelet and the newspaper article."

Mum smiles. "Well, I'm glad you've made a friend," she says. "Is he a nice boy?"

She's so annoying. She always does this sort of thing – changes the whole conversation. For a moment I think we're going to start arguing.

But then she says, "OK. Do you want to call or shall I?"

Heimlich manoeuvre

I don't want to call and I don't want to listen either so I leave Mum in the kitchen and run up to my room. Because Coral might not want anything to do with me or Mimi or any of my family. In fact, she might have left her phone number at the Sweet Suite so she can tell us to go away.

I look out of my bedroom window. The seagull's sitting on the flat roof. She looks up at me.

"Mum's speaking to Coral," I say. "Coral's still alive."

The seagull nods. Then she calls – *kee-yah kee-yah kee-yah kee-yah kee-yah kee-yah kee-yah kee-yah kee-yah kee-yah kee-yah*. Eleven times! I'm sure that was eleven times! I open the window and peer out. She's staring right at me.

"Is that you?" I say.

She tilts her head to one side. (It's her.) Then she calls – *kee-yah kee-yah kee-yah kee-yah kee-yah kee-yah kee-yah kee-yah*. Eight times. For a horrible moment I think she might be choking on a bit of plastic and I'll have to do the Heimlich manoeuvre. (Can you even do the Heimlich manoeuvre on a seagull?) But she looks absolutely fine. She doesn't look worried at all.

"What are you saying?" I whisper.

She shakes her head and calls again twenty times. Then she spreads her wings and flies up over the rooftops and out of sight.

I close the window and sit on my bed. I feel like Alice in Wonderland falling down the rabbit hole and ending up in a different world. Maybe the seagull's telling me that everything will make sense when I'm eleven or the twins are eight or in twenty minutes. Or maybe she's been kidding me all this time and when she sits on someone else's roof she calls a different number of times. Or maybe she's saying things are never as they seem.

Forever

It feels like forever before Mum comes up to my room. When she does she can't stop smiling.

"I just spoke to Coral!" she says.

She sits down on the bed beside me and gives me a hug. My heart's racing.

"She came into Brighton to do some Christmas shopping and saw your poster," she says. "She always looks in the shop when she's here. It reminds her of the Quartermans. She said it was the strangest thing to see a photo of herself in the window."

"What happened to her?" I say.

"The Quartermans adopted her," says Mum. "They had no children of their own so they were delighted to have Coral. She grew up in Eastbourne and years later the Quartermans moved to Brighton to open the shop. She had left home by then but she thinks they must have put the bracelet away in the attic and forgotten about it."

"Does she remember Mimi?" I say.

Mum shakes her head. "No," she says. "Not at all."

"Why didn't Mimi's mum look after her?"

"Mimi's mother was very poor," says Mum. "I don't think she could have brought up another child, especially a two-year-old. She had to earn a living."

It's so sad. I think Mimi's been missing Coral her whole life.

"Why weren't they told about each other?" I say. "They could have been friends."

Mum sighs. "This was seventy years ago, Iris. People did things differently then. They probably thought the kindest thing was to let Coral have a fresh start," she says.

"Does Coral have a family?" I say.

"Yes," says Mum. "And grandchildren. The youngest is a boy a couple of years younger than you. She sees him a lot. And she's got a little dog."

"Where does she live?"

"In a village not too far from here," says Mum. "Anyway, you'll be able to ask her these things for yourself. She's coming to Brighton at the weekend to meet Mimi. And you, of course. She'll be wearing a yellow coat."

"Like her cardigan?"

"What?" says Mum.

I shrug. I could explain about the yellow cardigan but I'm suddenly exhausted. I don't want to talk any more. I just want to sit very still.

Daydream

We sit together for ages while the sky outside grows dark. It's really nice. When Mum notices the photo stuck next to my bed she's surprised.

"Is that me?" she says.

I nod.

"I printed it with Mimi," I say. "It's my favourite. You look like you're daydreaming,"

Mum smiles. "Well, I did use to daydream believe it or not," she says. "I still do when I get the chance."

"Do you?"

She nods. "Oh yes."

The seagull flies back on to the flat roof and calls eleven times, then five times, then fourteen. She's definitely saying things are not always as they seem.

I lean my head on Mum's shoulder and close my eyes but as I do the quiet downstairs explodes into chaos. Pearl's screaming her horrible scream, Noah's shouting, "Not fair! Not fair!" and Mimi's singing "Truly Scrumptious" as loud as she can. Her voice high and strong.

Finding Coral

"We've got to get the Parma violets," says Mason. "We said there was a reward."

He's hopping along the pavement, seeing how far he can go without putting his foot down.

"But the person with information about Coral was Coral," I say. "She probably doesn't need a reward."

"A promise is a promise," he says.

He's beginning to wobble. He puts both feet on the ground.

"I wonder if she still looks like you," he says.

"I doubt it," I say. "She's seventy-six."

"I can imagine you as an old woman. You're already quite old, if you know what I mean."

I don't know what he means and I don't want to know either. I ignore him.

"Anyway," he says, "I've got something for you."

He reaches into his bag and pulls out the little fishing boat. He's painted it blue and white. New strings hang between the sails. It looks amazing.

"That's beautiful," I say.

"Thanks," says Mason. "You can give it to Coral if you like."

"You can give it to her yourself," I say. "You're coming to meet her, aren't you?"

"Am I?" says Mason. "Oh, OK."

He's grinning all over his face.

He puts the boat back in the bag and starts hopping again. This time with the other foot.

Not-Mason's-friend

Angie's wearing a Santa hat and standing on a step ladder hanging some baubles from the shelves. Customers are piling in, looking at the stockings full of sweets.

"Ah," she says, "Mason and not-Mason's-friend."

I wince. It's still so embarrassing. She doesn't mind who hears.

"We found Coral," I say.

"I know," says Angie. "Well done."

"And we need some Parma violets," says Mason. "For the reward."

"OK," says Angie, "help yourself."

Mason takes the jar to the counter and scoops some of the little sweets into a bag.

"By the way," I say (as quietly as I can), "I am Mason's friend now."

"Are you?" says Angie.

I nod. "Yes," I say, "so you don't need to call me not-Mason's-friend any more. If you don't mind."

"I don't mind," she says.

Mason gets some sticky toffee too and as we leave we each put a bit in our mouths. Then we walk home in silence, our teeth locked together.

Telling Mimi

We're meeting Coral today and I haven't told Mimi yet. I didn't want to worry her. But as we're having breakfast (baked beans and tinned peaches) I say, "We've found Coral. She's still alive."

Every emotion flashes across Mimi's face. One moment she's sinking, then she's flying, then she's lost her parachute, then she's found her parachute.

"I don't understand," she says at last.

"Everything you remembered is right," I say. "The boat did sink when Coral was two but Coral was rescued and someone adopted her. Your mum couldn't look after her so someone else did. And she moved out of Brighton."

Mimi looks like she's gone all the way out to sea and discovered she can't swim. She's searching for land.

"You didn't forget Coral," I say. "You didn't see her."

Mimi tries to smile.

"But you will today because she's coming to see you this afternoon. We're going to meet her on the beach. She'll be wearing a yellow coat."

Tears spill out of Mimi's eyes and sit on her eyelashes waiting to fall. And when she nods they do.

Coral

It's a cold white day. Coral's standing in the distance, an old woman wrapped in a yellow coat. A small boy like a stick figure spins round and round behind her. A little dog waits at her feet.

"There's Coral," I say.

Mimi laughs a strange painful laugh that seems to come from one of the seagulls overhead. Then she smiles. I put my arm through hers and Mum does the same, but Mimi pulls away and begins to (slowly) run, her hair flying behind her, a bracelet round each wrist.

Her scarf slips out of her hair and falls to the ground. Mason grabs it. And then me and Mum are running too in case Mimi falls (which she doesn't) and the twins think it's a race so they loop between us, squealing, and Dad and Mason pick up speed in case the twins fall (which they don't). And we all hurry along the front, past the West Pier, its skeleton rising out of the sea, the wind farm dissolving into the mist.

When she reaches Coral, Mimi hesitates for a moment, then she stretches out her hands and the two women step into the space between them and hold each other tight. They stand completely still for what seems like forever. The little dog yelps and the boy spins and spins, a dark outline against the white sky.

ACKNOWLEDGEMENTS

Thank you to those involved in keeping alive memories of the West Pier. The huge amount of information available has made writing this book a joy. In particular, I thank Brighton's West Pier Trust.

Thank you also to everyone I have spoken to about living with dementia – your stories have been an inspiration.

As always, many thanks to the wonderful team at Nosy Crow for your support and a huge thank you to Kirsty Stansfield for your advice, encouragement and, much tested, patience. Thank you also to my agent Gillie Russell for continuing to believe in me and to Rob Biddulph for another beautiful cover.

I would also like to thank Cath Howe and Helen Peters for chats, advice and those head in hand moments. Many thanks also to Sarah Wetherall for our wonderful, productive escapes to the country and to Mike Adams for friendship and conversations and for finding me a quiet place to work.

Finally, thank you as always to my family for your endless support and enthusiasm and most of all to Duncan for helping me wrestle clarity out of confusion. I couldn't have done it without you.

Also by S. E. Durrant

RUNNING ON EMPTY

"AJ's granddad was always the one who held the family together, so when he dies, AJ's world begins to crumble. He's just started secondary school and needs to make the cross country team to get one step closer to his dream of running in the Olympic Stadium, but he also needs to look after his parents who have learning difficulties. SE Durrant gives the reader a glimpse into the fragile life of a family held together by hope and kindness. A beautifully written and moving book."

The Scotsman

Read on for an extract from

RUNNING ON EMPTY

S.E. DURRANT

nosy crow

CENTRE OF
THE UNIVERSE

The most amazing thing I ever saw was Usain Bolt winning the 100 metres at the London Olympics. I was there with my mum, dad and grandad and we were high up in the stadium and I was seven years old and I felt like I was at the centre of the universe. And when he broke the Olympic record I thought the noise would lift the stadium up off the ground and catapult it right out into space. Because nothing about that moment felt ordinary.

And one of the most unforgettable things about it –

and not the best – was when people ran to the front and pushed forward for autographs, there was Amit from my class. He just popped up on the big screen. He was enormous. His head was the height of the high jump. He was trying to squeeze through to the barrier and he was just desperate to touch Usain Bolt or get his autograph on his ticket. And he did. He pushed right to the front.

I felt sort of annoyed. I hadn't even known he was there. I tried not to let it bother me but it did. And it's sort of bugged me ever since. I just had to not look too hard when Amit got right up close to Usain Bolt, and when he got his autograph I thought I'd be sick. I'm not kidding. I nearly threw up. I was thinking maybe I should run down to the front too and try to catch him when he did his lap of honour. He had the Jamaican flag round his shoulders and he didn't look in any hurry to get out of the stadium. But then I thought no, I might be too late. And it would be so embarrassing if I got caught on TV as the boy who tried to run down and couldn't get through. So I just sat there and Amit looked right into the camera and he was beaming from ear to ear like he'd just won the golden ticket in *Charlie and the Chocolate Factory*.

I would have done anything for that autograph and I still would, to tell you the truth, even though I'm eleven years old now. I tried to concentrate on what I already had, which I guess was something more spiritual. I felt like I had a connection with Usain Bolt and having Amit there sort of spoilt it. I think Usain Bolt probably felt more spiritual too. He was probably quite annoyed with all these people trying to get close to him, though he seemed to be quite enjoying it. He's good with the crowd.

Anyway, Amit got the autograph and I didn't and he took it to school at the start of Year 3 and did a talk about how Usain Bolt gave him a special look when he signed his ticket. It was sickening. But that's Amit for you. He's better looking and cleverer than everyone else and he always gets what he wants. I expect every school's got a kid like that.

And on the whole I've managed to turn that moment around in my head and make myself feel badly about Amit getting the autograph. I think, *Why couldn't he just stay in his seat and enjoy the moment? What was the matter with him?* It's funny how you can change the way you feel if you put your mind to it.

And the thing about that race is it really was special for me because the Olympic Stadium is just a few streets from our house. We saw them build it. Honestly. We're that close. And another reason it was special is Usain Bolt won in 9.63 seconds and Grandad lived at number

9 and we live down the road at number 63. I sometimes think if Grandad lived at number 8 Usain Bolt might have run 100 metres in 8.63 seconds and if Grandad had lived at number 7 and Usain Bolt had won the race in 7.63 seconds, the world would have physically exploded because it would have been a miracle. I know that might sound stupid but it's just a feeling I've got.

But usually when I think of Usain Bolt winning the 100 metres I think of Mum shouting at the top of her voice and Dad with his eyes shut and his hands over his ears and Grandad squeezing my hand and saying, "Can you believe it, AJ?" and me just knowing I would remember that moment for the rest of my life.